"Surprised to see me?"

"*Surprised* isn't the word for it," she muttered. But she couldn't help staring at him. The last time she'd seen Colby, he'd been a tall, lanky high school senior, the captain of the basketball team and adored by every girl at school—including her.

In fact, Colby, a close friend of her four older brothers, had been the unknowing target of her maturing hormones since she was twelve. To her youthful chagrin, though, he'd never seen *her* as anything but a target for teasing.

She studied him. In place of the young Colby she remembered stood a ruggedly handsome man who, if this hadn't been downtown Chicago, could have ridden in from the untamed prairie. He was dressed in jeans, a flannel shirt, leather jacket and worn leather boots. He'd doffed his Stetson and his lips were curved in a confident smile.

Rita met his gaze and asked, "So, why are you here?"

"At the moment, just paying you a visit," he said. "I dropped in on your mother the last time I was home, and when I told her I'd be passing through Chicago, she asked me to say hello. As for what comes later," he went on, with the same lazy smile that had thrilled her as a teenager, "well... that depends on you."

Dear Reader,

Most authors write a part of themselves into their stories. For the second book in my SULLIVAN'S RULES trilogy, I give you Rita Rosales, a heroine who—at one time in my life—could have been me.

Like Rita, I once dreamed of leaving home and going away to college to become a librarian. In this story, Rita not only becomes a librarian, she moves to Chicago to find excitement. In my case, life got in the way....

Fortunately, Rita and I ultimately both fell in love with—and married—the boy next door. We just went about it differently.

So here's to Rita, a woman who isn't afraid to dream the improbable dream and make it come true.

Enjoy!

Mollie Molay

Books by Mollie Molay

HARLEQUIN AMERICAN ROMANCE

HOW TO MARRY
THE BOY NEXT DOOR
Mollie Molay

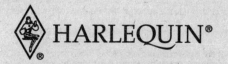

HARLEQUIN®

TORONTO • NEW YORK • LONDON
AMSTERDAM • PARIS • SYDNEY • HAMBURG
STOCKHOLM • ATHENS • TOKYO • MILAN • MADRID
PRAGUE • WARSAW • BUDAPEST • AUCKLAND

ISBN 0-373-75052-8

HOW TO MARRY THE BOY NEXT DOOR

Copyright © 2004 by Mollie Molé .

For Alan Steinhardt with love. He knows why.
And for Nicholas Steinhardt, the inspiration
for Lucas Sullivan's alter ego
in *Marriage in Six Easy Lessons*.

The woman who catches the bridal bouquet is destined to be the next woman to marry.

—An old proverb.

Chapter One

The sound of footsteps in the hall outside the office area drew Rita Rosales's attention away from her computer. She frowned. A check of her watch told her she was probably the only one still at work. Because of the rash of pre-Christmas sales, everyone who'd been able to leave early had gone, hoping to cash in on the bargains.

As the magazine's research librarian, Rita had been trying to finish her research notes on Chicago politics before the Christmas spirit completely overtook *Today's World* magazine, but she hadn't been able to concentrate for more than a few minutes at a time. It wasn't only the approaching footsteps that distracted her. It was the framed photograph on her desk.

She kept stealing glances at the picture, which had been taken a few weeks ago at the wedding of April Morgan and Lucas Sullivan. April was a colleague and her best friend, and one thing they had in common was their ability, thanks to the fact that both had grown up with older brothers, to recognize a "Sullivan man" when they met one.

A Sullivan man was the sort who acted on the rather old-fashioned chauvinistic principles espoused by Lucas Sullivan in his notorious article "The Mating Game," published some months earlier in *Today's World*. Dubbed "Sullivan's Rules" by Rita and her friends, the article was still stirring up a storm amongst its hundreds of disgusted female readers.

Which only showed, at least to Rita's way of thinking, that using rational thought in the mating game, as recommended in Lucas's article, was as wrongheaded as the other pragmatic theory of choosing a marital partner solely on the basis of his or her genes, ignoring sexual attraction.

For it was Rita's theory that sexual attraction was the prime factor in any relationship, a theory she preached but hadn't been able, in fact, to practice.

She scowled at the photograph. It showed her as April's maid of honor, holding the bridal bouquet, which she'd unexpectedly caught in the traditional toss. She didn't look happy about being the one to catch the tiny pink roses surrounded by delicate maidenhair fern, and she wasn't any happier now.

Not when she was all too aware of the superstition that the woman who caught the bridal bouquet would be the next to marry—something she would have yearned for if a man to whom she was sexually attracted had come along. But he hadn't.

April and Lucas Sullivan, seemingly the two least likely people to fall in love, had been a different story. When April, the magazine's senior features editor, had countered Lucas's six old-fashioned rules for how a man should choose a mate with six lessons of her own, all intended to enlighten Lucas about real women, the two had married. Obviously, Lucas had been enlightened.

"Rita Rosales?"

Rita started. Her fingers slipped from her keyboard. In the doorway, smiling at her, stood a man. Not just any man, she thought fleetingly. Without a doubt, he had to be the most attractive man she'd ever laid eyes on. It took her a moment to recognize him.

Her dormant hormones awakened with a start as she recognized the boy she'd had a crush on back home in Sunrise, Texas. He'd been the boy next door, and she hadn't seen him since the day he'd left for college and then become a Texas Ranger almost ten years earlier.

Only, from the way he'd grown up, it was clear he was no longer a boy.

And she wasn't a lovestruck teenager, either.

"Colby? Colby Callahan?"

"Yeah," he replied as he strode into her office. "Surprised to see me?"

The hairs on the back of Rita's neck began to prickle. A sure sign that something she might not like was about to happen. "'Surprised' isn't the word for it," she muttered as she again stole a glance at the photo on her desk. Was Colby's sudden appearance somehow tied in with her having caught the wedding bouquet?

No! Nobody really believed that silly superstition, did they? Certainly not her.

But she couldn't help staring at him. The last time she'd seen Colby he'd been a tall, lanky high-school senior, the captain of the basketball team and adored by every girl at the school. Herself included.

In fact, Colby, a close friend of her four older brothers, had been the unknowing focus of her romantic interest since she was twelve. But to her youthful chagrin, the boy next door had never seemed to see her as anything other than a target for teasing.

She studied him. In place of the young Colby she remembered stood a ruggedly handsome man who, if this hadn't been downtown Chicago, could have just ridden in from the untamed prairie. Dressed in denim jeans, a checkered flannel shirt, leather vest, bolo tie, leather jacket and worn leather boots, he looked as if he'd been born in a saddle. He doffed his Stetson hat, and his lips were curved in a confident smile. His brown eyes seemed to glow from within. She noticed the familiar small scar across his chin, the result of an unplanned collision during a championship basketball game. Instead of marring his features, the scar lent him an irresistible air of mystery and even danger.

Rita glanced out through the glass partition of her office to the surrounding area. As she expected, it was entirely empty. Certainly if Tiffany, the magazine's intern, hadn't left for the day, she would have floated into Rita's office with a look that said she was more than willing to get friendly with Colby.

Her gaze fell to the photograph once more. The coincidence of Colby's showing up when the superstition surrounding the wedding bouquet was on her mind made it impossible for her to ignore the uneasy feeling that there was a power operating somewhere she had no control over.

Hoping she was wrong, Rita met his gaze and asked, "So why are you here?"

"At the moment, just paying you a visit," he said, and the warmth in his tone took her by surprise. "I dropped in on your mother when I was home, and when I mentioned I'd be passing through Chicago, she told me to say hello. As for what comes later," he went on, wearing the same lazy smile that had thrilled her as a teenager, "that depends on you."

Rita bit back a tart response. Colby's suggestion that something might come later made her senses spin, and memories of her teenage years flashed through her mind. If her dreams had materialized, she would have become Mrs. Colby Callahan long ago.

But now, suddenly, she suspected that her mother had more than a little visit in mind when she suggested Colby say hello.

And the last thing she intended was to allow anyone, her mother in particular, to send her to the altar.

Her mother had already tried that. Not once, but twice.

Worried about her youngest child's marital future, Maria Rosales had been determined to see Rita married, in keeping with the family tradition of marrying young. She'd talked Rita into accepting the marriage proposal of an older family friend. A nice man, but not a man who stirred her senses.

She'd rebelled and decided to marry a college classmate. Two weeks later, realizing how mismatched they were, she'd broken the engagement, to both her intended's and her own relief.

Her mother made a second attempt to marry her off, this time to another family friend, a man even older than the first. By then Rita had obtained her degree in history and, asserting her independence, had flown off to Chicago to hunt for work. Now, as a respected research librarian at a reputable magazine, enjoying her freedom—though yet to meet a man she could love and respect—she had no regrets.

"I'm not sure what you mean by 'what comes later,'" Rita said, "but I'm pretty sure you've returned to your old ways." As a boy, Colby had delighted in teasing her and the look in his eyes told her he hadn't changed. "You might as well just come out and tell me what my mother *really* told you to do."

Trying to ignore the way her hormones were

jumping for joy at Colby's appearance, Rita casually pulled a strand of ebony hair away from her eyes and tucked it behind her ear. He could stop teasing her. She was a big girl now.

Her eyes widened when Colby strode to her desk, propped a hip against it and swept her with an admiring gaze. She had to fight the impulse to lean forward and raise her lips to meet his. To make at least one of her teenage dreams come true.

Before she had a chance to move or speak, he was the one to lean forward. He reached out a long, roughened forefinger and lifted her chin.

"I'm glad you seem to remember me," he said in a voice like a caress. "Since we're old friends, how about a real Texas welcome?"

Rita drew back, her lips tingling as if she *had* actually been kissed. She wasn't a lovestruck teenager anymore, she reminded herself. Nor, at twenty-eight, was she as naive as she'd been at eighteen.

"A real Texas welcome" was an enthusiastic hug and a big kiss. "Not on your life," she said. "You just can't show up and expect me to greet you like a long-lost friend. The last I saw of you was when you came to say goodbye to my folks—you barely acknowledged me. We're practically strangers!"

"I disagree. After all, I've known you and your family for years," he drawled lazily, his eyes fixed on her lips. "Besides—" now his gaze drifted down to the V-neck of her silk blouse "—in Sunrise, Texas, we're all practically kissing cousins."

He stirred as if he was about to take her into his arms.

Her fingers covering her tingling lips, Rita rose and stepped out of his reach before he could prove his point. "Kissing cousins?" she said scornfully. "I'll bet you don't even remember what I looked like ten years ago!"

"Sure do," he said as his eyes swept the rest of her. "You were one of those scrawny kids, all arms and legs, always tagging along after us boys. Of course, by the time I went away to college, you'd changed, but nothing like this."

It was clear he wasn't all that interested in the girl she'd been but rather the woman she'd become.

"I'm sure that's true of the entire female teenage population of Sunrise High School," Rita scoffed. "Besides, you couldn't wait to see the last of me back in Sunrise, so why are you interested in me now?"

When Colby's expression lit up suggestively, Rita wanted to bite her tongue. "Don't…don't answer that!" she stammered. "Besides, it really doesn't matter. Just tell me why you're here."

"That's easy," he said. "I've already told you that your mother suggested I visit you. She mentioned Christmas, said she hoped you'd come home for the holidays. Oh, yeah—" he paused briefly "—she also showed me a photograph of you."

"A photograph of me," Rita echoed. She pointed

to the framed photo on her desk. "This one, by any chance?"

Colby studied the picture. "Yeah, that's the one."

Rita began to regret the misguided impulse that had prompted her to send a print of the picture to her mother. She should have known her mother would have homed in on the bridal-nosegay superstition like a bear to honey. Rita's suspicion moved closer to certainty. She knew from experience how her mother's mind operated. Colby might not be aware of being manipulated, but her mother had obviously decided that Colby, family friend that he was, would make an excellent son-in-law, and was trying to get the two of them together.

She decided not to share that bit of information with Colby. She felt flattered that he now seemed to see her as a woman, but she wasn't about to open the door on the subject of matrimony with a man who'd strode in and out of her life as casually as Colby had. A man who, according to her brothers, dated many women but got serious about none. Yes, she felt the sexual attraction between them, but the man she finally chose would have to be special. A man who would love her and only her, treat her as an equal partner and be the father of her children. A loyal one-woman man.

Colby couldn't be that man.

"So," Rita asked, "what brings you to Chicago, anyway?"

"Got some business to do up here. Taking the time to say hello to you is no problem."

Rita wondered. Chicago was a long way from Texas, where Colby had been stationed, her brothers had said, somewhere along the border with Mexico. Whatever had brought him here had to be important.

"Well, I appreciate the gesture, Colby, I really do. But knowing my mother, sending you here to say hello and oh, by the way, see if I'm planning to go home for Christmas, isn't the whole story, is it?" she said grimly.

Colby mentally crossed his fingers and tried to think of a credible answer. He *had* promised her mother he'd try to persuade Rita to make the journey home, but he was reluctant to admit it. He sensed she hated being manipulated.

"Now, why wouldn't it be? Besides," he said with a teasing grin, "you're old enough to make your own decisions."

"Too bad my mother doesn't agree with you," Rita muttered.

"Don't you *want* to go home for the holidays?" he asked.

"No. Holidays or not, I intend to stay right here where I can run my own life. You can tell that to my mother the next time you see her."

Colby realized he'd inadvertently dropped into the middle of a Rosales family argument. Rita and her mother were two of a kind, both strong and stubborn women. He'd always admired strong women, but he didn't intend to get involved in their battles.

He would, however, have liked to renew his acquaintance with this particular woman. Too bad he was on a special undercover assignment, he thought as his body stirred in response to Rita's flashing green eyes and full moist lips. Now wasn't the time or place to renew their acquaintance in the way he wanted to.

As a lawman, he'd learned to play life's games with a poker face and to watch what he said. Considering the nature of the undercover mission he was on—helping to shut down the flow of illegal immigrants to Chicago—he couldn't afford to change his operating style now.

As far as anyone else was concerned, he *was* here to visit Rita. Keeping a promise to her mother to persuade her to go home with him for Christmas was incidental. He knew he could use this visit with an "old family friend" as a reason for being in Chicago. It was a good way to throw off anyone who might be following him. And after seeing how nicely Rita had changed, the plan was getting better all the time. A dinner date or two and he'd be gone out of her life.

He couldn't tell Rita the real reason for his being in Chicago. The knowledge might put her in danger.

He wondered about current difficulties between Rita and her mother. Knowing that Latina women tended to marry young and Rita was still single at twenty-eight, he suspected this was the crux of the problem. Her mother was undoubtedly anxious about Rita's lack of a husband. Rita, it seemed, had no intention of alleviating that anxiety. Which was fine with him. He had neither the time nor inclination to involve anyone in his dangerous profession—especially a wife.

On the other hand, it wouldn't hurt to renew his acquaintance with Rita. She was a beautiful woman, with a lush figure, gorgeous eyes, wonderful cheekbones and glorious long black hair. Why she wasn't already married beat the hell out of him. It didn't say much for the men in Chicago.

"Well, don't just stand there!" she said next, picking up April's wedding photograph and tossing it into the wastebasket. "If my mother actually sent you here to persuade me to go home for the holidays, just say so!"

"And if she did?" Colby asked cautiously, thinking that if she wasn't the only daughter in a family with four sons and other assorted male relatives guarding her honor, he would have taken her into his arms and kissed her sputtering protests away by now. A flesh-and-blood man could only stand so much.

Rita marched to her office door and held it open. "If she did, then whatever you had in mind to persuade me, you can forget it. I'm not going anywhere with you, and I'm certainly not going back to Sunrise. So do us both a favor and leave."

"Wait a minute!" Colby silently prayed to the god of fools to forgive him for the white lie he was about to tell. "All I did was drop in on your mother and she asked me to visit you. I never said she told me to persuade you to go home for Christmas. That was *your* idea."

"Fine then," Rita said coldly. "Now that you've visited me, you can go back to Texas."

"I can't, at least not today," Colby confessed. "Like I said, I have business that will keep me here for a few days."

Her eyes narrowed. "What kind of business?"

Colby thought fast. There was no way he could expose the sensitive nature of the undercover assignment he was involved in without coming out and confessing that one reason for showing up in Rita's office was that he needed an excuse for being in Chicago. He decided to sidestep her question. "Hey, aren't you worried about being here alone in the office at night? You don't know who might be in the building or what he might be up to. I mean, look how easily I talked my way inside." He glanced at his watch. "Isn't it time for you to go home?"

"Don't be ridiculous," Rita said. "I often work late when I have important research to do. Besides, there are guards roaming around who pass by every hour." She eyed him warily. "You must have given them a good excuse for letting you into the building. What was it?"

Colby shrugged. "I just told them the truth. That this is the Christmas season and I wanted to make a surprise visit to an old family friend. Since there's not much around here to steal, they let me in." He paused. "Anyway, now that I'm here, how about having dinner together and reminiscing about the good old days in high school?"

"What good old days?" Rita said. "You and I had nothing to do with each other in high school—you were three years ahead of me."

Colby didn't blame her for being skeptical. Maybe he ought to find a way to make his visit look like something more personal than just delivering a message from her mother. Now that he was here, there was no way he intended to leave without taking her out to dinner. Not when she'd grown into such an intriguing woman.

But faced with the seemingly impossible task of making friends with the grown-up Rita, Colby began to wonder how far and how long he could go before his deeply honed sense of honor took over. Forget her mother's expectations, he thought as he admired the girl grown into a tempting woman. How long would it take before he had to tell her the whole truth about why he was in Chicago, her mother's expectations excluded.

Even worse, now that he realized he was falling under the spell of Rita's fiery personality, there was more than one problem facing him.

The first was what her mother would say if she learned how easily he'd given up on his promise to persuade Rita to come home for Christmas.

The second and more immediate and important problem was the question of what Rita would think of him if she ever learned the other reason he'd looked her up.

Chapter Two

One valuable lesson Colby learned at the Texas Ranger Training Academy was that the best way to get people to talk was to share a meal with them.

Experience had gone on to teach him there was something intimate about eating together at the same table that loosened reluctant tongues. After all, he reasoned as he waited for Rita's answer, he'd used the method before while interrogating suspects and met with satisfactory results. Now was the time to find out if the same approach would work with her.

He'd have to coax her into letting him take her out to dinner. To get her to chat about her life in Chicago and at the same time make sure their past relationship, when he'd treated her as a kid, would stay in the past where it belonged. As for the future, he was sorely tempted to let it take care of itself.

"So how about dinner?" he asked again. "After all, it's the holiday season when folks get together, especially friends. Dining together will give me a chance to fill you in on all the things your brothers have been up to, as well. Then, if you want me to disappear, I promise I will."

To Colby's chagrin, the promise didn't seem to make a dent in Rita's resolve to be rid of him now. "I have a better idea," she said. "Why don't you just fill me in right now? Forget dinner."

"Come on, Ri, give me a break," Colby pleaded, deliberately using her childhood nickname. "Honestly, it's no trouble doing old family friends a favor," he added with what he hoped was a convincing smile. "Like I said, talking over old times might turn out to be fun."

"And like I said before, my old times didn't include you."

"Strange, but I can remember a few times when we had fun," he said, grinning broadly as Rita's eyebrows rose.

She didn't hesitate. "Name one!"

"I let you ride on the handles of my bicycle with me when all of us kids went down to the old swimming hole."

"That was fun?" Rita scoffed. "I distinctly remember falling off and skinning my knee. I didn't speak to you for a week!"

Colby winked. "The bike ride might not have been fun for you but it was fun for me. I remember your braids flying in the wind, tickling my nose and making me sneeze. That must have been why you fell off."

Colby might have chosen an innocuous incident to remember, but Rita felt herself thaw a little at the laughter she saw in Colby's eyes—and at the memory of how good Colby had looked in his cutoffs when they'd gone swimming.

If she wasn't careful, she'd fall for him all over again, so it was better to say no thanks. His ego might smart for a time, but at least she wouldn't be opening herself to temptation and its inevitable heartbreak. And from what she saw now, temptation was Colby's middle name.

Gazing at the mixed emotions crossing Rita's face, Colby realized he wanted to take her out to dinner regardless of whether the action misled his enemies. It had been a long time since he'd had the desire or opportunity to enjoy the company of such a lively and intelligent woman. And God, she was pretty. Why hadn't he seen ten years ago the beautiful woman she would become?

"Forget it, Colby," Rita said, all traces of warmth now absent in her face and voice. "We were kids back then, whatever happened in Sunrise years ago just doesn't count. So go ahead and tell me about my brothers, then leave."

Colby didn't respond, just remained sitting on the corner of the desk to wait for Rita to give in. "Since I'm not acquainted with Chicago," he said, "I'll even let you name the place."

He'd *let* her name the place? Rita bit back a sharp

retort. Colby reminded her of Lucas Sullivan and his six rules for a woman's behavior when interacting with a man she was interested in. Although, of course, she wasn't interested in Colby, she *was* interested in why he'd popped up so unexpectedly.

"Well, I suppose I can think of a good one. But there's something more going on here than a friendly visit, Colby," Rita insisted as she turned off her computer and made ready to leave. "I'm not sure what it is, but let me tell you, I'm not doing anything more with you than dinner. Got it?"

"Got it." In spite of their tenuous relationship, what complicated matters was the way Rita kept looking at him. He'd been in the playing field long enough to recognize mutual sexual attraction when he saw it. Still, given her fiery temperament, it might be wise to tread lightly.

"I'd be happy to tell you why I'm here, Ri," he said in the slow Texas drawl that made Rita's heart skip at the same time her blood boiled, "but I don't think you'll like it."

Rita frowned as she remembered the superstition surrounding the bridal bouquet. The farther away she stayed from Colby, the better off she knew she'd be. "The name is Rita now," she reminded him as she led the way out of the office. "Furthermore, I can read your mind like an open book."

Colby raised his right hand. "Dinner only, I swear."

"Okay," Rita replied. "But I'd still rather hear why you're in Chicago than talk about old times."

"You don't do much for a man's ego," Colby muttered. "Don't tell me you don't remember the high-school barbecue the year I graduated?"

Scenes of high-school celebrations flashed through Rita's mind. "Uh, vaguely."

"Vaguely? Sheesh. You mean you don't remember the kissing contest we had that night? Or the way all you girls lined up to kiss me?"

She burst out laughing. He was a tease *and* a flirt. "No, I'm afraid I don't."

"You really don't remember that when your turn came to kiss me, you threw your arms around me and kissed me so long and hard you won first place?"

"Ha. And here I thought you said I was just a scrawny kid whose braids made you sneeze."

Colby grinned wickedly. "True, but that was before I got a good look at you in that leather miniskirt and pink sweater."

Rita blushed. He wasn't making that skirt and sweater up. They had been her favorite outfit ten years ago. And he remembered.

Waves of heat rose through her at the sudden realization that he had felt at least some sexual attraction to her way back then. Back when she would have given just about anything to participate in a kissing contest with him. And what she knew now, heaven help her, was that the chemistry that had at-

tracted her to Colby all those years ago attracted her
now. The same heavenly brown eyes, albeit with attractive new lines crinkling at their edges. Wavy
brown hair, the cowlick over his forehead. And the
same killer smile.

Yet despite her attraction to the grown-up Colby,
despite her casual earthy chatter about sex being the
natural basis for a good relationship, she wasn't
about to act on it. At least not with Colby. She might
be many things, but she wasn't stupid.

And one of the things she was, was a virgin. The
virginal state might be unusual for a twenty-eight-
year-old woman in this day and age, she knew, but
the truth was that, even without her family's loving
and protective eyes on her, she'd never had the courage to practice what she preached.

When she did give up her virginity, she thought
with a frown, it wouldn't be with a man like Colby.
A man who collected girlfriends the way boys collected baseball cards.

As for her mother asking Colby to drop in and say
hello—and, she was sure, try to persuade her to come
home for Christmas—that sounded about right. Except, if she knew her mother, and she did, the visit
had a deeper agenda.

Rita thought of the wedding photograph showing her holding the bridal bouquet. Since her
mother was the most superstitious person she'd ever
known, and in southern Texas that was saying a lot,

had her mother decided Colby would make a good son-in-law?

Then again, maybe having dinner with Colby was worth the risk. Of all the men she'd dated, he was still the most attractive and intriguing. Maybe he *was* just being what they called back home neighborly.

Sure, and pigs could fly.

She eyed Colby's innocent expression. Her own intentions where sex in connection with Colby were concerned were shaky, but thank goodness, still firm. From the way he was looking at her as if she was good enough to eat, she wasn't so sure about his intentions.

"Well?" Colby prompted as they reached the bank of elevators. "Where to? We can go in my rental car."

She definitely needed someone to talk to.

"I'm still thinking," Rita said, her rational mind telling her to keep Colby at a distance while the irrational part wanted him close and personal. Very close. She hadn't brought her car to work today, because it was in the garage for an oil change and tune-up. It meant that she'd have to go with him in *his* car, which meant further uncomfortable closeness.

"Don't take too long," he answered with a smile that threatened to curl her toes. "I didn't stop for lunch on the way in. I'm starved."

His smile and the way he drawled the word *starved* was enough to remind Rita that Colby had charm to burn. That much about him hadn't changed.

Rita glanced at her watch. The only other person

with whom Rita felt she could talk about Colby and the way he was affecting her was the newly married April Morgan. A dedicated editor, April might still be in the building working. Now was the time to have someone talk some sense into her before it was too late. Who else but her best friend?

"Tell you what, I'd like to freshen up," Rita said as she tried a casual smile. "Why don't you go down to the café at the front of the building and have a cup of coffee or a soft drink. I'll catch up with you there in a few minutes."

Colby silently regarded Rita before he nodded agreement. Her excuse appeared to be genuine. Maybe, he thought with a hopeful surge of interest that continued to surprise him, her smile held a promise. Maybe, if he was lucky, there was a real Texas welcome in his future.

Still, he would have felt better if the smile that curved her lips had reached her eyes.

He'd been in and out of trouble before, and sometimes with women, he thought ruefully as he agreed to meet her later and entered the elevator. But for the first time in his adult life, he felt as if he were on probation.

APRIL WAS IN.

"Go with your gut instincts," she advised when she heard Rita's story about Colby. "First impressions are sometimes wrong." April's face lit up in a dreamy smile. "All you have to do is to look at the way Lucas and I met when I was assigned to be his editor. And what we went through over 'Sullivan's Rules.' Believe me, while I was teaching him a few rules of my own, it was touch-and-go. Thank goodness we finally realized there were lots of things we admired about each other."

"Yeah," Rita agreed. "I also remember it took less than twenty-four hours for you to actually fall for Lucas. Just look at what happened next!"

April looked pleased.

"Heck, that's no record," Rita went on. "It only took me twelve minutes this afternoon to realize I haven't forgotten how I felt about Colby."

April studied her friend. "Sounds promising to me. So what's the problem?"

"Colby's not a one-woman guy. He had scads of girlfriends when he was in high school, and according to my brothers, that hasn't changed. I find him sexy as hell, but I don't want to fall for a guy like that. He'd break my heart."

"Oh, Rita, honey. There must be something else you like about the man besides his sex appeal, or you wouldn't still feel about him the way you do," April said as she rummaged in her purse for her car keys. "Take it from me—it can't be only the physical side of a relationship women have to think about if we want to stay happily married. Besides," she added as she zipped her portfolio, "in spite of the earthy way you talk about sexual attraction, I think you do it just to shock people."

Unashamed, Rita grinned. "It does get their attention, doesn't it?"

"Yeah, but be careful," April warned. "Eventually there'll be consequences—and they might be unexpected! For instance, look at Lucas," she said as she led the way to the office door. "On the surface, he's a stuffy university professor with his nose always buried in some sociological study or other. Who would've guessed he'd turn out to be my sizzling hero? Give Colby a chance. Maybe he'll turn out to be yours."

"That's the trouble," Rita said. "Even as a kid, he was every girl's hero. Today, as a Texas Ranger, he's even more heroic, kind of a save-the-world type."

"Maybe he's the sort of person who likes taking care of people? Did you ever stop to think maybe that's why he became a lawman?"

Rita nodded. "Probably. Colby's late father was a Ranger, too. Colby was an only child and his mother doted on children so she fostered a lot of kids. After his father died in the line of duty, I remember Colby acted like a protective older brother to every single one of the kids as they passed through his mother's home on the way to adoption."

"Sounds as if he likes kids," April said. "Big point in his favor."

"I suppose, but his habit of protecting people is part of the problem, too," Rita said. "I don't want another older brother. As the youngest of five kids and the only girl, I always had someone telling me what to do. I know I should have been grateful, but I felt smothered. It finally got to the place where Mom's harping about my sticking to family tradition and marrying early and having lots of kids drove me away. That's when I left Texas. If I hadn't, I'd be married and living in Sunrise with three kids in tow by now."

"You do want children eventually, don't you?" April pressed the elevator's Open button.

"Sure. At least four, but not until I meet the right man, and I haven't met him yet."

"Not even Colby?"

"Especially not Colby," Rita said as she air-kissed April good-night.

If only she could believe what she was saying.

AN HOUR LATER, Rita found herself in La Paloma, an upscale Mexican restaurant.

The place was decorated to resemble a rain forest, and real palm and banana trees dripped glycerin raindrops. A beautifully decorated Christmas tree stood in a corner, gaily wrapped packages nestled in fake snow at its base. Mimosa bushes grew in large pottery containers. A water fountain, with a giant iguana as a waterspout, graced the center of the dining area, filling the air with a cool mist. The strains of "La Paloma," the song the restaurant was named after, mingled with the sound of chatter and laughter.

"Interesting place, isn't it?" she asked Colby as the scent of the sizzling fajitas that were being served at the next table made her mouth water.

"Very," Colby agreed, and held out her chair for her. "Actually, there's something about the atmosphere here that reminds me of you in that pink sweater and short leather skirt. Delicious and warm. I remember wanting to taste you and—"

"Stop right there," Rita said with an embarrassed look around her. "What if someone hears you?"

"Why?" he asked innocently. "What did you think I was going to say?"

Rita took a quick swallow of ice water, hoping to cool the sudden heat in her belly. "Forget it," she finally managed to say. "Why don't we talk about what you're really doing here in Chicago? Some business, you said."

Colby took a swallow from his own water glass.

"Yes, but the precise nature of the business I can't divulge." He made a show of unfolding his napkin. "I hope you're as hungry as I am." He reached for the menus and handed one to Rita.

"Hungrier," Rita said firmly as she glanced at the skillet of sautéed vegetables and strips of steak at the next table. The accompanying side dishes of sour cream, guacamole and salsa decided her. By the time the waiter set a covered plate of tortillas on the same table, she'd made up her mind. Before she was through with Colby, she not only intended to enjoy her dinner, she intended to leave him a bill large enough to remember her by.

"Fajitas are my favorite," she said to Colby. To the waiter who'd materialized at her side, she said, "I'll have a double order of the steak fajitas with all the trimmings. And a side order of fried plantains coated in brown sugar." She handed the menu to the waiter. "Oh, and a margarita, if you please."

Colby raised an eyebrow. "Are you sure?"

"I've been drinking for years," Rita said, looking at him meaningfully. "I'm not a kid anymore."

"I know," Colby agreed as he turned to the waiter. "I'll have the dinner salad, a peppered steak and a baked potato." He handed the menus to the waiter. "And a Coors Lite to go with it," he added with an amused glance at Rita. "It looks as if I'll be the designated driver tonight."

Colby waited until the waiter left before he sat back and studied Rita. He didn't know why she was blushing, but on her, pink looked good. As for her dinner order, with her trim figure, he couldn't imagine her being able to put away all the food she'd selected.

"Are you sure you're going to be able to eat all that?" he asked.

Rita gazed around the room before she answered. "I'm sure. If not, I'll take home the leftovers."

The waiter put their drinks on the table, together with a basket of toasted taco chips and a dish of salsa.

Even as Rita tried not to focus on his lips, Colby's

comment about his once wanting to taste her continued to boggle her mind. Had he really found her that attractive? She sipped the salted rim of her cocktail glass and dug into the corn chips.

"Another favorite of yours?" Colby asked dryly as she reached for yet another taco chip and dipped it into the salsa. He frowned when Rita seemed to spot something over his shoulder and her smile faded. The taco chip she'd been about to dip into the salsa fell out of her hand.

"What's wrong?" he asked quietly.

"I…I'm not sure," she stammered. "These two men just came in and sat at a table in the corner. They seem to be arguing, and one of them keeps staring at us."

Colby's pulse thundered. Damn! If he'd been found out this early in the game, he was in deep trouble. And, just his luck, at a time when Rita was with him.

He checked for the bulk of his gun, strapped to his left side under his jacket. Then he reached across the table and took Rita's hand in his. As if she'd just told him something funny, he laughed heartily, then said softly, "Look away from them and pretend to laugh at something I just said. When I say go, get up to leave. Just drop your napkin, pretend to excuse yourself and head to the ladies' room. No," he said between another laugh, "don't ask me why. Just get out of sight as fast as you can. Understood?"

Rita managed to break into a wide smile. "I don't

understand what's going on here," she murmured, "but don't worry. I'll do it."

"Good girl!" Colby nodded, waited another second, then at the sound of footsteps behind him, he said, "Go."

Rita shot a glance over Colby's shoulder and caught her breath. The swarthy man who had been staring at them had gotten to his feet and was striding toward their table.

The threatening look on the man's face as he approached filled her with apprehension. Since he was moving so fast, the idea of trying to find the ladies' room wasn't an option. But no way was she going to hang around. Without a second thought, she dropped to the floor.

Chapter Three

From where she crouched trembling under the table, Rita could see Colby's boots under the drape of the tablecloth as he jumped to his feet. She felt as if she was in a scene from an Al Capone movie. Certainly the city and the upscale restaurant were right, but this was twenty-first-century Chicago, where men were thought to be civilized, not Chicago of the 1920s.

Visions of Colby drawing a gun on the threatening stranger who'd been rushing toward the table only seconds earlier ago swam in front of her eyes. Expecting to hear gunshots any moment, Rita covered her ears and prayed.

But surely, a man trained as a Texas Ranger would have the situation under control by now, she thought. She closed her eyes, bit her lower lip and prayed she was right. Maybe it was just the vivid imagination she'd always been cursed with and teased about, but it seemed that the noises in the restaurant—the voices, the clatter of silverware, the music—had stilled. Had the other diners followed her example and hid under their tables in case all hell broke loose?

She heard feet rapidly approaching the table, held her breath and waited for the sound of Colby's voice challenging the man. Or, heaven forbid, the sound of gunshots. To her surprise, however, instead of stopping and confronting Colby, the second set of feet hurried on.

And to her relief, she could tell by Colby's feet that his stance relaxed. She let out a shaky breath.

A moment later, Colby lifted the tablecloth and regarded her solemnly. After a telling pause, he held out his hand to help her to her feet. "It's okay, Ri. You can come out now."

"What…what…happened?" Rita stammered as she took his hand and crawled out from under the table. She took a swallow of her drink and glanced around the dining room. To her surprise, only a few diners were looking at her curiously; the rest were acting as if nothing had happened. The soft music still played. The man who'd appeared to threaten Colby was nowhere to be seen. Neither was his companion.

To Rita's embarrassment, the waiter scurried back to the table.

She sensed by the way he looked at her that seeing a patron ducking completely under a table was a first for him. She didn't care. Dining with a Texas Ranger who wore a gun under his jacket and was able to calmly confront a man apparently set on murdering him was a first for her, too.

"Have you dropped something, ma'am?" the waiter asked, a look of alarm on his face. "I can get a flashlight and help you look…."

Rita managed a weak smile. "I dropped my napkin, thank you." She held it up for his view. "See, I've found it. But thank you for asking."

"Your dinners should be ready in a minute," the waiter said next. "Before I find out what's holding up your order, would you like a refill of your drinks?"

Rita nodded vigorously. She'd drained her margarita and was more than ready for another. She was still shaking with fear.

"Good idea," Colby said, "but not for me. I'm fine." He watched the waiter's disappearing back, then focused on Rita. After her reaction to what had fortunately turned out to be a mistaken case of danger, he realized that his plan to use Rita as a reason for his being in Chicago was a big mistake. He decided they'd have dinner together, then he'd be on his way.

"I hope you're not a poker player," he said, grinning. "You'd give yourself away every time."

Rita scowled. "It's not funny, Colby! No matter what you're thinking, I still think that man looked dangerous. From the way he came rushing our way, I was sure you were his target. I was afraid he was going to pull out a gun and shoot you. That was a reasonable fear, don't you think?"

"I think you've been watching too many late-night movies," Colby said in what he hoped was a soothing tone. "In case you're wondering what was going on up here while you were down there," he added with a wry glance at the hanging tablecloth, "nothing. Nothing at all."

"What about the way he was scowling at you?" Rita snapped. "That wasn't just my imagination. With four brothers always arguing over some stupid thing or another, I know an angry man when I see one."

"Maybe so, but I swear the guy ran past our table without even looking at me," Colby answered, laughter crinkling his eyes. "If you ask me, I'd say he desperately had to go to the men's room."

"The men's room?" For a moment Rita felt almost hysterical with relief. "Are you sure?"

"Looked that way. At least that's where he went after you disappeared." He flashed his killer smile. "You need to curb that imagination of yours. But don't get me wrong," he added as he reached over to sweep a wisp of hair away from her face, "I do appreciate the fact that you wanted to save me from harm."

The look of amusement in Colby's eyes took Rita back to the day ten years before when he'd stopped in to say goodbye to her brothers. She'd wanted to kiss him then and, heaven help her, she wanted to kiss him now. If she wasn't careful, she'd fall for him all over again.

Not a good idea. Especially if the disturbance to-night was an omen.

Rita took a deep breath. "Well, what did you expect me to do? Ignore an angry-looking man headed straight for your back? What would have happened if I hadn't warned you and it turned out I was right?"

Colby shrugged. The waiter reappeared, and with another wary glance at Rita set her refill on the table and disappeared again through the swinging doors to the kitchen.

"Well," Colby finally offered, "like I said, I appreciate your concern, but you don't have to worry about me, Ri. I'm always ready for trouble. As for what I would have done if you'd been right, I would have taken him down. It's all part of being a lawman."

He reached for his half-empty glass of beer and took a swallow. "I would have sensed something was wrong if we'd actually been in trouble."

"How could you have known what I was looking at? Your back was turned!"

"It's a sixth sense that all us Texas Rangers seem to acquire sooner or later," he explained. "Otherwise, I'm afraid I'd be a goner by now."

Rita's heart skipped a beat. She was amazed at how much she still cared about him. Apparently time hadn't made a difference.

As for Colby…did he care for her at all? Hardly, she thought as she returned the teasing grin that had driven her nuts back in Sunrise. He hadn't shown any real interest in her back then, so what made her think he cared for her now? Or that they could act on the surprising current of mutual physical attraction she sensed every time she caught him looking at her?

There was no use thinking about a future with Colby even in the unlikely event he asked for one, she told herself as she reached for a taco chip and dipped it in salsa. Colby was all wrong for her. She wanted a man with a nine-to-five job who'd be there for her 24/7. A man she could count on to stay alive to be a father to their children.

"So," she said brightly, determined to distract her mind from such thoughts, "about your conversation with my mother…"

With Rita's hands still trembling, he wasn't sure it was the time to tell her that her mother had asked, no, demanded, he find a way to persuade Rita to come home for Christmas.

He'd tried to beg off. Tried to say that corralling independent daughters wasn't in his job description. He'd never won an argument with Rita's mother when he'd been a kid and he hadn't won the argument with her last week. Instead, he'd made promises he wasn't sure he could keep.

Gazing at Rita, who was so much like her mother, he was beginning to suspect he wasn't going to win any arguments with her, either.

"Now look," he said casually, praying the waiter

would arrive any moment with their food, "your mother did ask me to say hello."

"Hello?" Rita gazed at him suspiciously. "A telephone call would have done just as well. Anything else?"

"Well, no—" Colby thought fast "—not exactly. Your mother asked me to give you a big kiss and a hug for her. But since you've already ruled out a Texas welcome for me, I guess I'll have to forget it, right?"

"Right," Rita said as the waiter approached their table with a sizzling tray of fajitas, a covered plate of tortillas and several side dishes—sour cream, guacamole and salsa.

Before she reached for a warm tortilla, Rita glanced at Colby. Maybe it was the margaritas, but suddenly a Texas welcome didn't seem like such a bad idea, after all. Especially when the hearty embrace would be with a grown-up version of the boy next door.

She tamped down the sensual thoughts that kept popping into her mind. "My brothers have said that your job as a Texas Ranger involves guarding the border. Anything else?" She carefully folded pan-seared red and green peppers and onions and strips of steak into a flour tortilla and, after due consideration, added heaping teaspoons of sour cream and hot salsa.

Colby shrugged as the waiter slid his order in front of him. No way was he going to spook Rita by telling her the truth behind his appearance in Chicago. Or to tell her of the time not too long ago when his partner had taken a bullet. He'd survived, thank God, but rehabilitation had taken months.

The past few minutes with Rita had been enough to convince him to keep the more dangerous details of his work to himself.

"No, that about sums it up," he said casually as he reached for his beer and took another swallow. "Nothing exciting."

She stopped in midbite. "Really?"

"Yeah. Nothing glamorous, that's for sure."

He lathered his baked potato with sour cream and added diced chives. "How about you, Ri? Your mom told me you're a research librarian for *Today's World* magazine. I picked up a copy at the airport. Great magazine. Keeping you busy?"

"As I said before, I'm researching Chicago politics. What's been more interesting," she added impulsively before she realized she was opening herself to the sensitive topic of marriage with the last man she should have opened her thoughts to, "is the debate over an article the magazine published two months ago—'The Mating Game,' or as some of us call it, 'Sullivan's Rules.' And, by the way," she added, "the name is Rita."

"Whatever." Colby put down his knife and fork when the topic of discussion changed. "Did you say 'The Mating Game'?"

The food in Rita's mouth suddenly turned to straw as she sensed Colby's surprising leap of interest. Then again, the subject *was* enough to pique anyone's interest, male or female. The big increase in magazine circulation since the article had been published was ample proof. "I can give you a brief rundown of the article, but only," she added reluctantly, "if you're really interested." She hoped he wasn't.

Colby's lips twitching made her wonder if he was laughing at her. "Sure. I'd like to hear."

Rita gulped. No way could she discuss male-female relationships with a man who sent her hormones into overdrive. She tried to dissuade him. "You'll only be bored."

"Try me," he dared with that killer smile.

Doubtful of his academic interest in the subject and convinced he was teasing her, Rita took another sip of her margarita for courage. "Well, since you asked," she began, "it seems there are three theories about what makes up the attraction between the sexes. But then," she added when his eyes seemed to twinkle knowingly, "you're probably already aware of them."

"Nope. 'Fraid not," he said annoyingly. "Actually, it's not a subject I spend much time thinking about. Why don't you enlighten me?"

Rita glanced around at the surrounding diners and lowered her voice. Sullivan's Rules was hardly a safe dinner topic with a man who affected her the way

Colby did. She fixed him with what she hoped was a pragmatic look and soldiered on. "Okay. For one, there's the survival-of-the-fittest-theory about how you subconsciously choose a mate with good genes to pass to your children."

"You do?" Colby's eyebrows rose to his hairline.

Rita blushed. "Not me!" she protested. "I meant 'you' as in most people."

"Interesting," he said thoughtfully. "So, you said there are other theories?"

Rita took a deep breath. "Yes, there's Sullivan's Rules. It's a sociological study that the author of the article, Lucas Sullivan, came up with. Lucas maintains the mating game is, or should be, a question of rational thinking based on the social compatibility between the sexes."

Colby's eyebrows knitted in interest. "Go on."

"Sullivan maintains there are six rules women must follow if they want to interest a man. In my opinion—" she paused before he could comment "—and before you have something complimentary to say about the rules, in my opinion they're all hogwash."

"Really? Hogwash, huh?" Colby said with a teasing grin. He couldn't seem to help himself, Rita thought. Old habits not died hard, and she was leading the way. "You said there were three theories," he reminded her when she frowned at him. "What's the third one?"

Rita almost choked on her margarita. "Are you sure you want to hear it?"

"Definitely," he said. "In fact, I can hardly wait."

"True love," she said faintly.

"You don't say. Now that's a term that covers a lot of territory." He paused. "Sounds as if a woman came up with this last theory," Colby said dryly. "True love. Is that all there is to it?"

Rita cringed inwardly. She wasn't going to tell him her not-so-private theory was that pure sexual attraction was the driving force between men and women. Or that she was waiting for the right man to come along. The last thing she wanted was to give Colby any more ammunition to tease her with.

"Like I said, the term word 'true love' takes in a lot of territory," Colby said as he went back to his steak. "Are you sure you can't be more specific?"

Rita sipped her margarita again and waited for the courage to talk sex with Colby.

"It's not actually a scientific theory. Just an observation of mine." She dipped another toasted taco strip into the salsa.

"Ah. So it's *your* theory. Sounds as if you don't believe it. Care to share?"

"Not tonight," Rita answered primly. The food she'd eaten lay like a lump of lead in her stomach, and her head began to ache. She'd never been much of a drinker, despite her airy assertion earlier that she'd been drinking for years. When Colby's image started to blur, she decided she wanted to excuse herself and go home to sleep off her headache.

But to her dismay, she spotted Tom Eldridge, the owner and editor in chief of *Today's World,* waving at her from across the room. Seconds later, he was at her table. With him was a well-known talk-show guru who regularly contributed to the magazine. *Oh, no.*

"Hi, Rita! Good to see you!" Eldridge gestured to his companion. "Rita is a research librarian for our magazine, Paul. Rita, you've heard of Paul Horton, right?"

"We haven't met, but yes," Rita said as she peered at the two newcomers. Horton was the host of a live talk show in which he visited controversial topics, usually with guests he pulled from his audience. What was he was doing with Tom? The answer was sobering. His presence had to be about the controversial Sullivan's Rules. Damn!

She glanced at Colby, who'd risen to his feet and was patiently waiting to be introduced. "Sorry," she said, gesturing to him. "This is Colby Callahan," she said. "Colby is an old friend of mine from Texas."

"So, you're a friend of our Rita," Eldridge said as he shook Colby's hand. "What brings you to Chicago?"

Rita frowned as she listened to their exchange. *Our Rita?* Sure. Tom was a typical "Sullivan." And from everything she'd seen of the man, Horton wasn't far behind.

With that expansive false grin creasing his face, the man nailed more than one misguided female program participant to the wall with his patronizing attitude. If *she* was ever invited to be a guest on his show she'd tell him what she thought of him.

She cringed as Colby chatted with the two men. From the friendly tone of the conversation, it looked as if they were kindred spirits and fast becoming friends. Sullivan men all. She realized this was the first time she'd classed Colby that way, and the thought depressed her. She was reluctant to examine why.

"Mind if we join you?" Tom asked when the conversation wound down. "Paul here has an interesting idea I'd love to run by the two of you."

Rita peered at Colby over the rim of her cocktail glass. She sensed the worst was yet to come.

Colby shrugged. "Sure. Why not?"

Rita said nothing.

"So where in Texas do you hail from, Callahan?" Horton asked as he sat down and signaled the waiter.

"Sunrise."

"Sunrise?" Horton frowned. "I've never heard of the place."

"It's a small town near the Mexican border," Colby explained and downed the rest of his beer.

"Yeah, and the most exciting thing that happens there is the train going through on its way to Galveston," Rita muttered into her empty glass.

Horton's eyebrows rose, and Rita realized her mistake. He'd sensed there was a story somewhere in her remark. *Small-town girl in a big city?* Huh. Nothing new about that. Maybe he'd give it a miss.

It seemed he had, at least for now, for he turned back to Colby. "So what do you do in Sunrise, Callahan?"

"I don't live there anymore," Colby explained with a glance at Rita. "My job takes me all over Texas."

"Oil?"

"Nope."

Colby's obvious reluctance to admit to being a Texas Ranger finally penetrated Rita's haze. She didn't know why he didn't want people to know his profession, but she sensed it had something to do with his presence in Chicago.

She'd been right about Colby, she thought as she digested his vague answer. Colby had to have had some ulterior motive in looking her up. His drop-in visit was no accident, even if their history went back a long way.

She'd tried to save Colby from an irate diner before. Now she had to save him from Horton.

"I want to tell you how much I admire your TV show, Mr. Horton," she said, her voice dripping honey. "I try to watch it whenever I have time. Tell me—" she smiled "—how do you manage to come up with such fascinating and controversial topics?"

Horton's smile grew. He obviously felt flattered. "Life itself is controversial, don't you think?"

As if impressed by his wisdom, Rita nodded.

Horton went on. "For instance, take any two people, put them together on a desert island, and you'll find they have plenty of things to argue about, right?" He laughed without waiting for an answer.

Rita's gaze met Colby's. She could see gratitude to her in his eyes, even as he nodded his agreement.

Good grief! That they were both thinking along the same lines at the same time took Rita by surprise. Could she and Colby actually be on the same wavelength, after all?

No way.

"Oh, I don't know about that." Rita felt she had to disagree if only to take that smug smile off Horton's face. "Men and women would never get together long enough to have children if all they did was argue." She was astonished to see Horton's face light up.

"Ha!" Tom exclaimed. "That brings me to the reason Horton and I are together tonight." He glanced at Horton. "Go ahead, Paul."

"The number of irate letters-to-the-editor over Lucas Sullivan's study in your magazine," Horton said, "begs for a confrontation between a man and a woman. On my show. I've inquired if Sullivan himself would be willing to do it, but it seems he's only just gotten married. He and his new wife are too busy working on a follow-up study to have time to become involved. To top it off, and I know you're not going to believe it, folks, the man's wife was his editor! I guess they're too in love to argue."

Rita glanced at Tom Eldridge. Had he told Horton that she and April were best friends? She decided not to enlighten the talk-show host.

Before she could challenge Horton about his attitude, the waiter arrived to take orders for drinks, and the moment was lost. Colby said, "Sounds as if I'm going to have to get my hands on that issue of your magazine, Eldridge. Rita was just explaining to me before you arrived that there are several popular theories on the subject of the mating game, or," he said with a nod at Rita, "Sullivan's Rules. I'd be very interested in reading the published article."

Horton's lips widened in his trademark expansive grin. "I'm sure Tom will be happy to see that you get a copy tomorrow. When you've read the article, give me a call." He fished in his pocket and handed Colby his card. "I'd be interested in hearing what you have to say. Maybe you and Rita here would like to debate Sullivan's study on my show next week."

The waiter arrived with their drinks. When he put a fresh margarita in front of Rita, she smothered a groan. She'd not only lost a chance to tell Horton what she thought of his patronizing attitude, one more drink and she'd be under the table again.

As for debating the mating game on television with Colby, Horton didn't know it, but the chances were slim to none.

She intended to tell him so as soon as her head cleared.

BLEARY-EYED, RITA GAZED around her. She was sitting in Colby's rented car, the engine running, in the restaurant's parking lot. For the life of her, she couldn't remember how she got here. She recalled taking a swallow of her third margarita. Judging from the throbbing of her head and the way the scenery was swaying, that last drink had been a mistake. An improvised ice pack made of a towel wrapped around ice cubes was sitting on her head. And Colby…Colby was taking her shoes off!

"What in heaven's name are you doing?"

"Awake now, are you? I'm just trying to make you comfortable," he said soothingly. "Take a few deep breaths, hold that ice pack in place and try to relax. You'll feel better in a few minutes."

Rita obliged, and the pounding in her head dropped a decibel. "How did I get to your car? I don't remember."

"I carried you here, darlin'. You were in no shape to walk on your own."

Rita moaned and shifted the ice pack to another throbbing area of her head. "I had too much to drink. I've never done anything so stupid in my whole life."

"Not to worry. Turn around, maybe this will help." Colby sat down beside her and gently massaged the base of her neck and her shoulders. "The Christmas season's probably affecting you. Maybe going home to Sunrise for Christmas is a good idea, after all."

Rita slowly shook her head. "Mom would only try

to talk me into staying." Colby's fingers continued to do their magic. "Uh… I didn't do anything to embarrass myself, did I?"

"I guess that depends on how you look at it." He gave her shoulders a final pat, then sat back and grinned.

"Look at what?" She peered at Colby. "For heaven's sake, tell me. Apart from drinking that third margarita, what else did I do?"

"You volunteered to be on Paul Horton's TV show next Thursday night."

Chapter Four

"I volunteered to be on Horton's TV show?" Rita echoed, horrified. "No way! I can't stand the guy. He's another Sullivan.

"A Sullivan, a male chauvinist, a controlling guy." Rita scowled as she tried to process Colby's bad news. "That man thinks he knows everything there is to know about everything and everyone—especially women."

Rita became aware that Colby's hand was adjusting the collar of her coat, which was jammed uncomfortably against her skin. When his fingers brushed the skin of her throat, she shivered, but not from the chill. She hunched her shoulders and leaned away from Colby's touch. His touch felt too good to bear.

"So, this Horton is a Sullivan kind of guy?" Colby asked.

Rita took another deep breath as she regarded the amused expression on Colby's face. "Yes. For that matter, so is Tom Eldridge. But at least he keeps it pretty much to himself. And he *did* bring April and Lucas together."

She was about to suggest that Colby qualified as a Sullivan, too, considering how he'd hit it off with Tom and Horton. Then she reconsidered. She had a hazy recollection of Colby and her connecting briefly tonight, of their being on the same wavelength. So instead, she complained, "You could have stopped me before I made a complete fool of myself and agreed to Horton's proposal, couldn't you?" She re-adjusted the ice pack. Her head was throbbing anew.

Colby looked surprised. "I figured you knew what you were doing. I didn't realize you were so out of it when you took Horton up on his offer. And when you agreed to his follow-up suggestion, too."

Rita stared at Colby. "What suggestion? What did I agree to?"

Colby shrugged. "You agreed to find a guy to de-bate the Sullivan six-rule article with."

"Oh, no!" Rita wailed. "Please tell me I didn't. Please tell me you're only teasing."

"I'm afraid I can't, Ri." He sounded genuinely sympathetic, and she warmed to him a little. But then he ruined the moment with his usual teasing. "Amazing what you do after only three cocktails. I wonder what you might do next."

"Colby!" she sputtered. "You know me better than that."

"Well, no, actually, I don't. I know little Ri from

Sunrise, Texas. As for the grown-up Rita—" his gaze swept her face "—it's a different story. You're definitely not a kid anymore."

Despite the pain in her head, Rita felt another pleasurable shiver. Oh, dear, she thought. She mustn't let him get to her so easily. Maybe it was just her weakened state.

"If it will make you feel any better," he went on, "Horton offered you five thousand dollars if you would appear on his show with a partner of your choosing. Your boss jumped in and offered to sweeten the pot if you agreed. Heck," Colby added with a speculative look, "I'd be willing to chip in myself in order to see that performance."

"Five thousand dollars is a lot of money for an hour's work," Rita said, then the reality of finding a partner and debating the meaning of love in terms of a relationship before a television audience sank in. "Oh, no," she wailed again.

"Horton suggested me as your partner," Colby said modestly. "I told him I was interested but not available."

Rita was speechless.

Just then, the parking attendant ran up to the car. Colby rolled down his window. "Pardon me, sir, has the ice pack helped the lady? Would you like more ice?"

Rita wanted to sink under the seat.

"No, we're good," Colby replied. "Thank you."

He peeled a bill off a wad of cash he'd had in his wallet and waved him off.

At the moment, Rita felt too miserable to think any more about what she'd agreed to. "Please take me home," she said after the attendant moved off.

"Sure thing," Colby agreed. "Home it is."

Rita found herself listing to the left and leaning against his shoulder. She wasn't prepared to admit it, but she was grateful for his solid strength and his reassuring attitude. Maybe she was going to survive, after all.

"Wait a minute, you don't know where I live!" she said as he put the car in Drive.

"So tell me."

She did, then added, "I'll give you directions as you drive."

Before he turned onto the street, Colby briefly dragged his right arm across her shoulder. "Don't worry, Ri," he said gently. "Things will look better soon. I've discovered you're quite a woman."

Rita had learned something about Colby tonight, too. Teasing aside, he was the kind of man who could make a woman feel cherished. She was almost able to forget that after tonight they might not see each other again. But that was what she wanted, wasn't it? Or did she?

They drove along Lakeshore Drive to her upscale apartment overlooking Lake Michigan. She hated to admit it, even to herself, but Horton's offer would go a long way toward solving her financial woes. Her job, as much as she loved it, did not command a very high salary.

Colby glanced at Rita as he drove. "Are you sure you're okay? You're very quiet."

She sat up straighter, and Colby found that he missed the warm feel of her against him. "Just worried that I might have said something else back there that I wish I hadn't."

Colby thought there was no way he could sit so close to Rita and ignore the sensual stirring in his body. Good thing she'd sat up.

"Don't worry," Colby said to take his mind off thoughts he knew he had no right to pursue. "If anyone behaved like a fool tonight, it was me. I should have known better than to let you have that third margarita."

Rita didn't answer, and he wondered if she'd invite him into her apartment for coffee before he said good-night. No, he decided. She obviously needed sleep more than she needed to hear him say goodbye.

He glanced at the twinkling lights that had turned Lake Michigan's dark waters into a diamond-studded mirror. The sparkling water and the brilliantly lit buildings rimming Lakeshore Drive were beautiful. So different from Texas's dry border country.

"I must have been blind in high school not to have known how lovely you would look all grown-up," he said. *He wasn't blind now.*

"I guess I have changed a little," she replied with a sigh. "Turn left here."

"You sure have," he agreed as he made the turn. He meant it. She was beautiful, and sensuous and fiery. He wished he could wrap her in his arms all night....

He gave himself a shake.

Rita was still the girl he'd grown up with. The kid sister of his four best friends. And he'd promised Rita's mother he'd try to persuade her to go home to Sunrise for Christmas.

But more important, he had a dangerous mission to accomplish. Instead of using a visit to Rita as an excuse to be in Chicago and possibly putting her at risk, he had to find another reason to stay for a few days, a week maybe. And then, after he met with the local and federal authorities to compare notes, he planned to return to Ranger headquarters in Waco, Texas.

Seducing Rita was a definite no-no.

"Headache gone yet?"

"Not really." She seemed to give up trying to sit straight and cuddled into his shoulder. Colby shifted uneasily as the closeness made his body stir again.

One minute Rita was insisting she was a grown woman and wanted to be treated like one. The next she was burrowing into his shoulder as if she were a child.

He felt Rita shudder against him. "What is it?" he asked.

She sat straighter once more. "I just realized I

couldn't take Horton up on his offer even if I wanted to. What if my family saw me on TV? Oh, turn right here. This is my street and that's my building there." She pointed at an elegant three-story Victorian. "I live in the second-floor apartment."

"Your family would be proud of you," Colby said. "Not everyone gets a chance to appear on television. It's not a bad way to earn a sizable chunk of change, either."

"Yeah. That's almost four months' rent," Rita agreed. The thought of earning enough money to pay the rent for the next few months made her feel better. All she had to do for the debate was be her true self and avoid the topic of the importance of sex in a relationship. Discussing heterosexual relations and the nature of love shouldn't be a big deal. The bigger problem was the man she had yet to come up with to debate her.

Arthur, the office gofer? No. He was so shy he'd trip over his tongue.

One of the men on the office baseball team? Heck, if they couldn't get a pitch across the plate, how would they be able to handle a debate?

Colby drew up in front of her building and parked under a streetlight. "You've got one of those cow statues on your front lawn, too," he said with a grin. "I swear," he added as he came around to open the door for her, "there have to be more cows in Chicago than there are in the whole state of Texas."

Distracted by the curve of Colby's strong jaw, where a faint five-o'clock shadow had begun to appear, Rita said, "Uh…our cows are only plaster. Yours are real. The kindergarten class in the school down the street decorated our cow for us."

"That explains the blue nose," he laughed. He held out a hand to help her out of the car.

"I can do this by myself, thanks."

Colby smothered a grin. "Rita, you've still got the headache and you're dead tired. It won't hurt to accept a little help. In fact, you'd better let me help you upstairs."

"If you insist," she said primly.

"I do." With that he swung her up into his arms and settled her head against his shoulder. "My hands are busy. Better grab your handbag."

Rita frowned. He might be helping her, but he could at least have given her the option of refusing. If she hadn't sensed it before, she knew it now. Colby was a true Sullivan.

He carried her to the front door. "You can put me down now," she said as she fumbled for her house key. "You needn't see me inside. I feel much better now."

He waited for her to unlock the door. "I still haven't given you that Texas welcome hug your mother sent you."

Her key in the door, Rita frowned. "I don't remember you saying anything about a hug. I distinctly heard you say she asked you to say hello. Are you sure?"

"Just my luck," Colby answered with an exaggerated sigh that told her he was kidding. "You don't
seem to remember something as important as a kissing contest. But how can you forget a simple request
from your mother?"

Rita cocked her head and traded looks with Colby.
"There was no kissing contest," she said as her mind
began to clear. "And I'm quite certain you never mentioned a hug-you message from my mother, either."

Colby sighed. "She'll be terribly disappointed in
you when I tell her you refused."

Rita pushed open the door of the house, stepped inside, threw her coat on a hall tree and turned back to
confront Colby, who'd followed her in. "For heaven's
sake! As long as you put it that way, just give me the
hug. I wouldn't want to disappoint my mother!"

When he hesitated in the doorway, she moistened
her dry lips. "Well, what are you waiting for? It *was*
a hug you wanted, right?"

Taken at his word, Colby thought fast. He didn't
quite know what there was about Rita that had made
him come up with the idea of a hug and a kiss, but
he definitely wanted to taste her inviting lips before
he parted.

His desire and his integrity were at war with each
other. A white lie had a time and a place as long as
it didn't hurt anyone. Considering that Rita appeared
willing to act out the hug with him, that time and
place appeared to be now and here.

She gazed up at him, her lips parted, her eyes sparkling with an emotion he wasn't sure he could read.

"Well?" she demanded, her arms open wide. "Are you just going to stand there, or are you going to stand and deliver?"

Colby threw rational thought to the night winds. He placed his hands on Rita's waist and, eyes locked with hers, slowly drew her to him until they were mouth to mouth. Smiling into her beautiful green eyes, he bent and kissed the lush lips he'd been dying to kiss from the first moment he'd walked into her office.

"Oh, my," Rita said when he drew away to give her time to breathe. "Maybe you were right, after all."

"Right about what?" he murmured as he eyed Rita's slender neck and toyed with the idea of nuzzling the hollow of her throat.

"About the kissing contest," she said, smiling. But he heard the breathlessness in her voice. She was as excited by the caress as he was.

"Let's try that kiss again—see if we'd still win the contest," he said. Despite his teasing tone, his suggestion was dead serious and he put action to the words.

"You may be right about the hug, but I'm sure it wasn't from my mother," Rita said when she came up for air. Then she leaned against Colby's chest and listened to the rapid heartbeat that echoed her own. His warm breath tickled her ear. She raised her arms, put them around his neck and pulled his face down to hers. "Kiss me again so I can make sure, please."

Colby laughed, then did as she asked. If there had been a kissing contest, they would have taken first prize.

Finally able to kiss him the way she'd dreamed of doing since they were teenagers, Rita stopped thinking about Colby's intentions and kissed him with all her pent-up emotion. Whatever he'd been as an eighteen-year-old, today he was all man, and she felt like the sensual woman she'd been saying she was.

If only there was something more between them than this powerful physical attraction.

If only Colby lived in Chicago.

At last Rita took a step back. "Knowing how old-fashioned my mother is, I'm sure she didn't send you here to give me a hug and a kiss. Unless…" Rita studied Colby.

Colby gently outlined her tingling lips with a forefinger. "Unless what?"

Rita thought of the wedding photograph where she'd held April's bridal bouquet. "If my mother actually asked you to do anything, I'll bet it was to bring me home to get married."

Colby looked startled. "Huh? You're getting married?"

"No. But my mother thinks my catching April's bridal bouquet is an omen."

"Who's the lucky guy?"

Colby might not believe it, but Rita was sure her mother had Colby in mind for the groom.

Just as she was sure it was now time to say goodbye.

She held out her hand. "Thank you for a lovely evening. With the exception of the time I spent under the table, I really enjoyed having dinner with you."

Colby glanced over her shoulder. "No invitation to come inside for coffee?"

Rita felt her face heat. If she let Colby into her apartment tonight, considering the way she felt, chances were he wouldn't leave until morning. She shook her head.

"All right," Colby said reluctantly. "I guess it *is* time to say goodbye." He grasped her shoulders, leaned forward and dropped a warm kiss on her lips. "Thank *you* for a lovely evening. Sweet dreams, and I hope they're about me." He winked as he turned and left.

FIRST THING THE NEXT MORNING, Rita was in April's office with Lili, the magazine's graphic artist, in tow. "The two of you have got to help me decide what to do about that man!"

"What man?" A dab of pastel watercolors from the project she was working on remained on Lili's chin.

"Colby Callahan, that's who!" Rita related everything that had happened from the time he'd appeared in her office doorway late yesterday afternoon to the moment at the door to her apartment last night.

By the time Rita finished, Lili's eyes were shining. "Oh, my goodness! Then what did he do? Did you ask him inside?"

"I wanted to, I really did, but after the way I reacted to his kiss, I was afraid to."

"And then what happened?"

"He actually said goodbye and left. But not before he kissed me on the lips again, winked and told me to dream about him."

"He didn't!" Lili gasped.

"He did. I swear, the man's ego is as large as the State of Illinois!"

Lili sank into a chair and sighed. "You are lucky, Rita. Just imagine, an old flame of yours has turned into a romantic hero—a Texas Ranger. How romantic! You must persuade him to be your partner on the television program," she added. "By the time you get through discussing the meaning of love, the man will have to realize he really cares for you."

Just then the office gofer rolled his beverage cart to the door of April's office before Rita had a chance to reply. "Coffee, doughnuts, anyone?"

"No, thank you, Arthur," Rita said when April looked tempted. "Maybe later."

He looked at her and grinned. "Yeah, but I wanted to tell you that Alice and I are engaged. I'm going to put a down payment on a ring as soon as I get my next paycheck."

"Good for you," Rita said as she turned the cart around. "Why don't you come back later."

"Sure thing," he replied happily as he pushed the cart out the door. "Since April is a newlywed, maybe she can give me some advice."

"I'm sure she'll be happy to, but later." Rita closed the door behind him. "Now, back to Colby. I was asking you to help me make up my mind about Horton's TV show," Rita said helplessly. "I could call him and tell him I've changed my mind. But I sure could use the extra money, so maybe I *should* do it—just not with Colby."

"I thought you told us Colby turned down Horton's offer."

"He did. It's just that I have a strange feeling about him. The way he turned up so surprisingly in the first place gives me a weird feeling he'll turn up again. And I'm not sure I want to get further involved with him."

"You don't?" Lili asked. "It sounded as if you liked the way he kissed you good night."

"Yes, I did," Rita agreed with a sigh. "I just don't want to encourage him. I have this strange feeling there's something more going on here than he says."

"I don't know what you're so worried about anyway, Rita," April broke in. "Have you looked in the mirror lately? Really looked? Colby would have to be blind not to see how gorgeous you are. I'd say if you have even a smidgen of interest in him, and I

know you do, find a way to get him involved in the
TV program."

Rita shrugged helplessly. "Maybe. But unless
Colby has changed, he has a dozen women back in
Texas waiting for him."

"Then get to him first. You'll not only make five
thousand dollars, you might even get your man."

"I'm not sure I *want* to get him," Rita replied.
"Besides, it could be too late."

"Oh! Well, if Colby really isn't interested, just
what kind of man does this Horton guy want you to
team up with, anyway?"

"Give me a minute." Rita reached into her slacks
pocket. "He sent me a fax this morning telling me the
sort of man he expects me to find." She read off the
fax. "'Single. Between the ages of thirty and forty-
nine. Good-looking, strong, intelligent. Preferably
employed in a man's world. Good sense of humor
and able to take it on the chin, as well as give it
back.'"

Her eyes widened as she studied the fax. Horton
had met Colby only last night, but he'd somehow
managed to describe the man she'd remembered.
"Colby would be perfect, but I think persuading him
to appear on TV isn't going to be easy. He said he
wouldn't be available. And last night he said goodbye, not good night."

"If I was able to change Lucas's mind about those
silly mating-game rules of his, I'm sure you can bring

Colby around," April said. "My sincere advice is go for it."

Rita cringed inwardly. Her friends thought she could use sexual attraction to help get her man, which, of course, she'd implied with all her talk about sex being the basis of a good relationship. They didn't know she planned to save herself for marriage.

Chapter Five

Rita made tracks for Tom Eldridge's office the following morning before the mail was delivered. Appearing on Paul Horton's popular TV show and debating the meaning of love might be the last thing she would normally want to do, but the chance to earn five thousand dollars was stronger than her pride.

Asking Colby to partner her was out; she didn't know how to reach him, anyway. After last night, he'd vanished as abruptly as he'd appeared. She explained this to Tom and said that if Horton wanted Colby to partner her on his TV show, he'd have to find him for himself.

"This show is so right for you, Rita," Tom said. "I've heard you're a woman of strong opinions and have no qualms about expressing them."

Rita blushed at the thought of just what opinions of hers Tom was referring to. Her playful talk about the importance of sexual attraction? Well, she thought as she took a deep breath, she only had herself to blame.

"I do have a question, though," she went on after a cautious look around to make sure no one was within earshot to hear her make a fool of herself. "Why me?"

Tom steepled his fingers and regarded her benevolently. "I'm inclined to believe that since he wasn't able to get Lucas in person, Horton wants to hear your interesting slant on those six rules of Sullivan's."

"My slant?" Rita scowled at Tom's use of the word *interesting* in connection with her slant on sex versus Sullivan's Rules. "Horton's got the wrong woman. My only connection with Lucas is April. I wish she was appearing on the show with Lucas."

Tom shrugged. "I understand he tried and they declined. All I really know is Horton got the idea to ask you when I happened to mention you were a good friend of April's."

"That's the only reason?"

"I think so. After all, since those rules have the whole town on its ear, I figure Horton must have figured you were close enough to April and Lucas to have some insight into how Lucas came up with those six rules of his."

"You can say that again. Lucas didn't know what he was talking about," Rita muttered. "The female half of the mating game, anyway."

Tom raised a questioning eyebrow. "You included?"

"You bet! Any sensible woman would resent having an academic tout those ridiculous rules for a man finding a mate."

Tom beamed. "That's the kind of talk Horton's looking for. If he can't have April and Lucas, I guess you're the next best thing. He told me that a woman with strong opinions is exactly what makes you a good subject to spice up his program."

He chuckled as he picked up the issue of *Today's World* with Sullivan's mating-game article featured on the cover. He kept it on his desk. "If you think of what Sullivan's Rules have done for our circulation, you can imagine what they will do for Horton's program."

Rita shifted uneasily as the enormity of what she was agreeing to sank in. "Well, just so you know, anything April might have told me about how she brought Lucas around to her way of thinking is confidential. You can tell Horton to avoid that topic or I'm not going on his show."

"Show," Tom echoed with a broad smile. "I've watched him on TV once or twice and that's exactly what it is, by God. By the time he gets through goading the participants, the whole hour turns into a sideshow. Although," he added thoughtfully, "I can't say I can find any fault with Paul's method. He's already risen to number six in the ratings."

Rita worried her bottom lip. She might not approve of Horton's methods, but five thousand dollars was too great to resist. "Okay, but let's get this straight. I don't intend to talk about Lucas Sullivan or his rules."

"Maybe you won't have to. Horton's also mentioned a discussion on the meaning of love. But," Tom added with a grin, "if he doesn't bring up Sullivan's Rules somewhere during the program, I'll eat my hat."

"He won't do it with my help!" Rita rose to her feet, planted her hands on her hips and glared at Tom. "First of all I'm single. I intend to *stay* single until I find the right man, and I don't mind saying so on Horton's program. So, in spite of the rumors you might have heard about my take on sexual attraction, I'm probably the last person in the world to discuss the meaning of love. Especially in the way Horton would like me to. As for Sullivan's article and those six rules of his, Horton wouldn't want to hear what I really think."

"I'm not sure what you're referring to," Tom said, "but you're still a woman. Like all women, I'm sure you have some experience and opinions on love and marriage."

"Opinions, yes. Experience, no," Rita said before she could stop herself. She knew from the look on Tom's face he didn't believe her.

Tom shrugged. "Whatever. I'm still hoping one thing will lead to another and Sullivan's rules for the mating game will come up during Horton's show. When it does, we can jump on the publicity his program generates to keep the circulation pot boiling. Even have Lucas write another article. In fact, I've already had numerous requests from other magazines for permission to print excerpts from Sullivan's article."

Rita bit back a caustic comment. It was easy to agree with Tom's reasoning. The dollar signs floating around Tom's head were clear. She couldn't blame him. She was in it for the money, too.

"Now, about Horton finding the man to debate with you," Tom continued. "I agree that the man with you the other night, Colby Callahan, is just the right guy," he said, disregarding the fact that no one knew where he was. "There's something written all over Callahan that says he's a man's man. That kind of guy is bound to have a few strong opinions about women."

"Yeah, I know what you mean. He's a Sullivan," Rita muttered, stopping short of adding, "like you."

Thankfully, Tom's phone interrupted him before he had a chance to continue arguing with her. "Sure thing," he said into the phone after listening for a moment. "You can refer to the Sullivan article in your newspaper as long as you don't quote the article verbatim. And by the way, you might want to listen to Paul Horton's television show Thursday night. You might find it interesting. Yes, there's a connection, and no, that's about as much as I'm able to tell you at this time."

Rita groaned at the reminder of her future involvement in Horton's TV program. "Getting back to what Colby thinks about love and relationships…well, that's precisely the point," she said when Tom hung up. Goaded into sounding off by the grin on Tom's face, she went on, "You and Paul Horton are cut from the same cloth—you're both Sullivans. You're both men who not only think you know all about love and marriage, you believe you're God's gift to women."

Tom threw up his hands. "Sorry, count me out. I'm not interested in finding a wife. Besides, Sullivan's Rules have me convinced. Just keep on sounding off like that when you get on Horton's program. That's just the stuff he's looking for!"

To Rita's chagrin, the angrier she became the happier Tom looked. "I wouldn't ask Colby to appear on the program with me even if I knew where to find him. I'm not even sure I'll ever see him again. He's another Sullivan. Tell Horton to find someone else and call me when he does!" Rita sniffed and made for the door before she said something she'd regret.

Later came too soon.

"WELL, I WAS BEGINNING to think you weren't going to stick around long enough to do us any good," Lieutenant Bruner of the Chicago Police Department grumbled. He was the head of the operation Colby had been sent to assist. Bruner motioned to a chair.

Colby grimaced. "Got a little sidetracked," he said as he dropped onto the chair. "I'm here now. What's going on?"

"Status quo. The illegals from Mexico are still

being funneled to Chicago, and we're still chasing them," Bruner replied, "but I'm more interested in what sidetracked you."

"I guess you might say it was the girl next door," Colby admitted. "She lives in Chicago now. I only meant to drop in to say hello to make it look as if I'm merely here for a vacation, but one thing seemed to lead to another."

"I assume that the girl next door has become an attractive woman? Attractive enough to interest you?"

"Afraid so," Colby confessed. "But that's over."

Bruner leaned across the desk. "Maybe, maybe not, but it *is* a damn good cover. Just watch your back."

THE NEXT DAY, Paul Horton's secretary called Rita to make an appointment for a preshow conference. "You'll be happy to know we've found someone to partner you on our telecast," Helen added briskly.

"Who?" Rita asked with a defeated sigh. "Knowing something about the guy might make it easier for me to talk to him later on the program."

"'Easier' is not the operational word here," Helen replied. "Besides, if I told you, that would ruin the surprise. We've scheduled you both for next Thursday evening. I know that's short notice, but if you have any questions, feel free to call me. If not, we'll see you next Thursday afternoon around two. We'll introduce you then."

Rita rubbed at the knotted tendons at the back of

her neck as she murmured her agreement. The news that Paul Horton had moved so quickly to find someone willing to discuss the meaning of love, instead of Sullivan's Rules, hadn't come as a surprise. Love was always a hot topic. It was the slant Horton intended to put on it that troubled her.

No matter who her partner turned out to be, she decided she was going to speak her mind and say exactly how she felt about love and marriage. Her folks back in Sunrise were going to be proud of her, but her friends…well, they were in for a surprise.

After preaching about sexual attraction to anyone who'd listen, she intended to tell the truth as she really saw it. Sex merely for pleasure was out. Sexual activity within marriage, on the other hand, was definitely in.

Believing in remaining chaste in today's open society might make her seem odd, but she didn't care. With her own mother and father as role models in a marriage that had lasted more than forty years to show her the meaning of true love, she intended to follow their example.

In the meantime, she couldn't help wondering what kind of man Paul Horton had managed to dig up.

THURSDAY AFTERNOON Rita was in Horton's office ready to meet the man he'd found to partner her on his show. Ten minutes after Helen Arkin ushered her into what she called the greenroom, where her boss and the man in question were seated, deep in conversation, Rita realized she wasn't ready, after all.

"Colby?"

He smiled, stood and strode to meet her, taking her cold hands in his. "Funny the way you keep being surprised when I turn up. By now I'd have thought you'd gotten used to seeing me around. But yes, it's me."

Rita glanced at a grinning Horton and at his clearly smitten secretary. "I know why *I'm* here," she said with a cool look at Horton, "but what are *you* doing here? I thought you weren't going to be available. I assumed you went back to Texas."

"Nah," he said with his trademark grin. "I've just been too busy to call. If you remember, I told you I had some business to take care of while I was here in Chicago."

"How nice you could find the time for the show." Her words dripped with sarcasm, and Rita snatched back her hands before he could give her another one of his Texas welcomes. In his beige slacks, cream-colored shirt open at the neck, and dark brown jacket and cowboy boots, he took her breath away. How in the world was she going to be able to discuss the meaning of love with a man she'd been crazy about since puberty?

"I thought Callahan was the best man to partner you on the show tonight," Horton said with a grin that made her blood boil. "It didn't take a rocket scientist to sense the sexual tension between the two of you the other night."

Rita shot Colby a cool look. To her annoyance, Colby merely shrugged.

"When I gave Colby here my business card," Horton went on, "I was hoping he'd get in touch with me. He did. Actually," he said with an approving glance at Colby, "with Callahan's strong masculine persona I had a gut feeling I'd be able to use him on my program sooner or later. I got lucky," he added with a wink. "Sooner came before later."

Masculine persona! Rita thought darkly. As if Colby's ego wasn't inflated enough.

"Not with me as his partner," she retorted. She hitched the strap of her purse higher on her shoulder. "I'm outta here!"

"Come on, Ms. Rosales, you don't mean that."

"There's no way I'm going to go on television with that man," Rita said. "If you want me, you'll have to find someone else. And as for you," she said to a grinning Colby, "well, find some other woman to torment." She started for the door.

Horton called after her and motioned to his secretary, who handed him an envelope. "First of all," he said, "it's too late for you to back out now. The program starts in a few hours. If you'll just stop to think objectively, I'm sure you'll change your mind." He waved the envelope at her. "Hell, five thousand dollars isn't hay."

Colby reached for Rita's elbow when Horton was through talking and drew her aside. "Hang on a moment, Rita," he said with a quelling glance at their host. "Horton is right. Besides, I swear I'm harmless. I volunteered to partner you on the telecast not only because I knew you were reluctant to appear on the program, but because I figured it would be easier for you to talk to me than to a stranger."

"So you can boast?"

"No. To be honest," he added with a hint of laughter in his voice, "this isn't going to turn into another story about old times. We're adults now. Besides, I really would like to hear your take on the subject of love."

Rita regarded him warily. Why Colby wanted to discuss the meaning of love with her when they hadn't spoken to each other for years, except for the other night, of course, was beyond her. But then, she thought with a delicious shiver, there *had* been that Texas-welcome exchange in the entry hall of her apartment house. And who knew what else he might have in mind that could be just as enjoyable. "What do you really know about the subject of love?"

"Not much," he confessed with an unrepentant grin as he brushed her cheek with the back of his hand, "but I'm sure willing to learn."

"Not from me," Rita retorted when the hairs on the back of her neck started to tingle. "I'm still Ri, my brothers' little sister. The kid who lived next door. What makes you think I'm experienced?"

"Come on, Rita," he apologized softly. "I never said you were. I just remembered you used to have an opinion on everything back in Sunrise. I just thought you might have an interesting opinion on the subject of love, too."

Hardly mollified at the reminder she'd always been outspoken, Rita shook her head. "You'll have to do better than that if you want to convince me."

"How about if I figured that by partnering you on Horton's show, I would be keeping my promise to your mother to look in on you while I was in Chicago."

Rita sniffed at the reminder of just how well Colby had kept his promise to look in on her. "You're doing this to keep a promise? Ha! First of all, you've already done that. And then you disappear without even telling me you're going?"

"It was business," Colby said, pleased to learn Rita had missed him. He couldn't tell her he'd been checking out clues that might lead to the masterminds behind the trafficking of illegal immigrants from the Texas border to Chicago. Not without blowing his cover, and sure as heck not without frightening her.

He'd learned a hard lesson the other night at La Paloma. Using Rita as a reason for being in Chicago was out. She was not only busy imagining that danger surrounded him, she actually feared for his life. That put hers in jeopardy.

For sure, he thought as he smiled invitingly at Rita, things had changed for him the moment he'd walked into her office. If she'd looked so striking at dinner the other night, today she was even lovelier in her short, fitted forest-green suit and a frilly lime-green blouse that brought out the bewitching clear green of her eyes. The grown-up Rita was a sensual and appealing woman. But considering his under-cover mission and his ties to Texas, falling in love with her was out. She had a life in Chicago.

"By the way, you look great," he said softly. "The audience is going to love you." He tucked her hand under his arm and slowly drew her back into the room.

"Hey, wait a minute!" Horton surged to his feet. "Hell, Callahan, if I'd known you were going to get cozy with Ms. Rosales, I wouldn't have invited you on my program. How am I going to get a rise out of you if the two of you are so damn agreeable?"

Cozy? The memory of Colby's lips on hers flashed through her mind again. The way his tongue had thrust into her mouth and the way his arms had crushed her against his hard body had gone beyond cozy. Her body suffused with heat. Even as she'd had to force herself to remember that, for her, sex only went with marriage.

"There's really no problem," Rita finally said with a sidelong glance at Horton intended to placate. "Colby has always teased me. We knew each other years ago, but no matter what it might look like, I can assure you we're practically strangers now. As for our having opposite opinions about the meaning of love," she added, ignoring Colby's raised eyebrows, "I don't think that's going to be a problem."

"Fine." Horton handed Rita the envelope. "I expect a good performance from the two of you tonight. Helen will brief you later so that you'll have a heads-up on what to expect." He glanced at his watch. "Since I want your performance to sound spontaneous, there's not much more I'm going to tell you. We go on at eight. You might want to take a break and be back here by seven."

Colby waited until the door closed behind Horton and his secretary. One way or another he had to make his peace with Rita before he headed back to Texas Rangers headquarters. After all, she was the innocent party to his deception. "How about a late lunch?"

Rita shook her head. "Thanks, but I'm not hungry. Actually, my stomach is tied up in knots from just thinking of going on TV." She rubbed her stomach. "In fact," she muttered, gazing at the envelope she held, "I keep wondering how I got myself into this mess."

As for Colby, if he hadn't believed in fate before, he did now. Her flashing eyes and shapely body, coupled with her keen mind, had awakened sensual thoughts that continued to surprise him.

He had to face facts. He'd been too wrapped up in his career to notice how quickly time was passing, or to dwell on the reality that little girls could grow up to become beautiful women. He was thirty-one, unmarried, and although he had a number of foster siblings he kept in touch with, he had no real family of his own.

He didn't know if it had been the lecture from Rita's mother about the importance of marriage and family tradition, but he knew that having a foster family spread all over the map of Texas wasn't enough for him. Maybe it *was* time to start thinking about a family of his own.

But Rita? He'd always thought of her as a kid sister, that is, if he'd taken the time to think about her at all. Now, as he watched her mentally wrestling with herself over having agreed to appear on TV tonight to discuss the meaning of love with him, he realized he sure wasn't thinking of her as a kid sister now.

No, he told himself again as they left the studio; he had no future with Rita. He had plans to return to Texas as soon as his mission was accomplished. From what Rita had said about going home for Christmas, she clearly felt she belonged in Chicago.

"How about an early dinner then, and a little friendly conversation?" He spoke lightly despite the depressing thought that tonight was going to be the last time he'd see Rita for some time, if ever. "For old times' sake, I'd like to think we parted as friends."

Colby was right, Rita decided. She'd made a commitment and she had to deliver. She had to appear on Horton's talk show with Colby even if it killed her. She'd take him at his word that he didn't know zip about the meaning of love.

Even so, he sure knew a lot about a Texas welcome. And what she'd felt at his touch had nothing to do with friendship. She might not have much experience, but she recognized sexual desire when she encountered it.

"Okay," she finally said, ignoring the strange pangs of loss and regret. "A goodbye dinner and a few hours of conversation before the show sounds fair enough. I know of a small place around the corner that specializes in good old-fashioned American cooking. Something you ought to appreciate."

"Lead the way," Colby said. "I'm all yours."

But not for long, Rita thought wistfully.

MELVIN'S DINER, a distinctly traditional eatery, boasted a menu Colby's grandmother would have approved of. After glancing around a room decorated for Christmas with green and red crepe streamers, a miniature Christmas tree and sprigs of mistletoe, Colby chose a booth at the back of the room where he could keep an eye on the door. This time, he made sure Rita sat beside him, not across the table.

After the way Rita had reacted to suspected danger the other night, he intended to see what was going on around them.

"I don't need to read this—I already know what I want to order," Rita said as she handed Colby the menu. "My favorite is the meat loaf and mashed potatoes."

"No fajitas tonight?"

"No," Rita answered with a shrug and a winsome

smile that reminded Colby just how enchanting she was. "When I'm in La Paloma, I go Mexican. When I'm here, I go Midwestern."

Colby glanced at the menu and tossed it aside. "You can count on my being a steak-and-potato man no matter where we go." He beckoned to the waiter.

The hint that they might be having dinner in the future took Rita by surprise. "I take it you're a man who dislikes changes," she said as she gazed into Colby's warm brown eyes, the scar on his chin and at the endearing smile that curved his lips.

"I never really thought about it until now, but you could be right," Colby said as he impatiently brushed back the shock of hair over his forehead. "I suppose it's because of the foster kids my mother took in when I was a kid. The household population was always changing, and I can still remember having a hard time feeling sorry seeing them having to leave."

Rita opened her mouth to answer, when she seemed to freeze. "What's wrong?" Colby asked. "Something I said?"

"No," Rita murmured. She was staring through the large window at the front of the diner. "I just saw the same two men from the other night at La Paloma across the street. And this time," she added grimly, "neither of them appears to have the men's room on his mind."

"Are you sure it was the same two men?"

"Very sure. In fact, I think they were standing there watching us for the last few minutes."

"What exactly did they look like?" Colby asked as he took a quick glance out the window at the empty sidewalk. "Take your time. Try to remember every detail, okay?"

Rita shivered. "One was dressed in the same black suit he wore the other night. The other man was dressed like a cowboy, only this time he was wearing a cowboy hat with a red feather tucked in the hatband."

Colby glanced out the window again. The men sounded normal enough, except for the red feather that he knew by now was a gang symbol.

"I think you're mistaken," he said. He didn't want to worry Rita, but considering the reason he was in Chicago, he couldn't deny *he* was worried. "Wait here. I'm going out there to take a look."

"No, Colby. Stay. Please."

Colby's lips tightened. "It's all right. I'll only be a minute."

With Colby gone, Rita glanced uneasily around the diner. The lunch hour was over and the dinner hour was still a couple of hours away. She and Colby had the place to themselves. The only problem was that since Melvin's was a no-frills restaurant with no fancy white tablecloth, she had no place to hide.

To her relief, Colby strode back into the diner within the promised minute. "Whoever was out there, they're gone now." He slid into the padded seat beside her. "Like I said the other night, maybe it was your imagination."

"I know what I saw—" Rita scowled "—and what I saw was a repeat of the night at La Paloma. There *were* two men out there watching us, and one of them *was* the man you decided needed to get to the men's room."

Without comment, Colby signaled for the waiter again. Glancing at the window to make sure no one was looking into the diner, he ordered the meat loaf special for Rita and a rare steak and baked potato for himself.

"Dessert?" the waiter asked. Rita shook her head.

"Come on now," Colby chided. "In an all-American diner like this one, you have to order apple pie, preferably with ice cream."

Too upset to eat, let alone treat herself to her favorite dessert, Rita silently shook her head.

"You'll feel better soon," he said reassuringly, mentally kicking himself for considering using Rita as the reason for being in Chicago. If she was right about the men, he owed her, big time.

He made a mental note to make sure Rita would have some kind of protection while he went back undercover tomorrow.

Their dinners arrived, piping hot, looking and smelling good enough to make his mouth water. "Go ahead," he said, nudging Rita's plate filled with meat loaf, mashed potatoes and gravy and fresh green peas closer to her. "You'll feel better if you have something in your stomach."

Rita's stomach rebelled at the thought of food. Still, it appeared Colby wasn't going to start until she did, so she picked up her fork and made a pretense of eating.

She thought of how Colby had been back in high school. A daredevil looking for trouble. Tonight, as she had in La Paloma, she had an overwhelming feeling that this time trouble had found him.

Chapter Six

Waiting in the TV station's greenroom for the call to go onstage for Horton's show, Rita felt a hollow in her middle that meat loaf and mashed potatoes hadn't helped.

The sound of heavy equipment being moved outside the door, together with voices shouting instructions, was disconcerting. Hurried footsteps and a muffled curse when a heavy object fell did even less to calm her apprehension at appearing on television with Colby. The old adage that the anticipation of trouble could be worse than the trouble itself afforded little comfort.

"Coffee?"

Rita looked up. Colby stood there smiling and holding out a steaming cup of coffee as if nothing out of the ordinary had happened an hour ago. Easy for him, she thought. He was used to being in danger. He might not have believed he'd had a problem back at Melvin's Diner, but she was convinced that someone was lying in wait for him. He was a target, and unless he was lucky, it was just a matter of time before he was hit.

"Thanks." Rita took the coffee and stared gloomily at the hands of the large wall clock relentlessly marking off time until doomsday. Even the Christmas tree in the corner with gaily wrapped gifts under it couldn't lift her spirits. How was she going to get through the next two hours knowing Colby would be exposed to a studio audience, a member of which might be carrying a concealed weapon?

It didn't make her feel any better to know that Colby still thought there was no threat, that she was a victim of her imagination.

Colby sat down beside her. "You look worried. Is it the thought of dealing with Horton before a live audience?"

"No, not really," Rita answered, trying to switch her thoughts from the unthinkable to the present. "The day a guy like Horton or anyone else has me tongue-tied will be a cold day in hell."

"Attagirl!" Colby said admiringly. "You never took anything from anyone when you were a kid and it looks as if you haven't changed." He paused. "But something's bothering you, Ri. Please tell me. Maybe I can help."

"You don't want to hear it," Rita muttered, "and you've got to stop calling me Ri. The name's Rita."

What was the use of telling Colby she feared his life was in danger? She knew he didn't believe it.

"I guess you're more anxious about your television appearance than you thought," Colby said into her silence. "Either that or you're still worried about what you think you saw back at Melvin's."

"Right! Colby, I know what I saw—those men were watching you through the diner window! It wasn't my imagination, no matter what you think!" She gestured wildly with the coffee cup.

Colby grabbed the cup out of her hand before the coffee spilled on the floor. "Rita, the only reason you keep imagining someone is after me is because you know I'm a lawman. Forget worrying about me. This isn't Texas, this is Chicago!"

"Yeah, right," she said with scowl, "and you're only here in Chicago because my mother sent you to persuade me to come home for Christmas. You *did* say you had business here, and since you're a lawman, the business must have something to do with criminals, right? And criminals can be dangerous, right? So…" She ran out of steam.

Colby sighed, took the last swallow of his coffee and threw both paper cups into a wastebasket. Maybe it *was* time to tell her the whole truth. To tell her that by being seen with her, he was "hiding in plain sight." Knowing the Rita of Sunrise, she'd bawl the hell out of him, but she'd eventually forgive him for using her that way.

The problem was, would he ever be able to forgive himself?

"You're right, Rita," he began. "I—"

"It's time for Makeup to do Ms. Rosales," Horton's secretary, Helen, said, tripping into the room. Helen frowned at the sight of Colby sitting so close to Rita.

"I don't think Mr. Horton would approve of your being so friendly at a time like this," she said. "Do try to remember that for the next hour you have nothing in common with Mr. Callahan, Ms. Rosales. Don't forget that you agreed to take opposite sides on the topics you discussed during your interview with Mr. Horton the other day at La Paloma." She glanced at her notes. "Perhaps you need a reminder," she went on. "The topic tonight is the meaning of love."

Rita wasn't surprised at the way the secretary glanced admiringly at Colby while at the same time chastising her for being too cozy with him. Women had always fallen for Colby from the first moment they laid eyes on him. Apparently they still did.

"As for you, Mr. Callahan," Helen added with a smile of approval, "your turn in Makeup is next. Now," she said with another glance at her notebook, "it says here you'll be leaving Chicago shortly. Mr. Horton has asked me to thank you in advance for taking the time to appear on his program." She turned to Rita. "Now, Ms. Rosales, please follow me."

Rita sobered at the secretary's reminder that

Colby would soon be heading back to Texas. A state she'd left for good when she'd declared her independence. Now that Colby the man had appeared in her life, she was beginning to think leaving Texas was not such a great idea.

With a lingering glance at Colby, who gave her a thumbs-up, Rita slung the strap of her bag over her shoulder and reluctantly followed the woman who had just reminded her that while she and Colby might be friendly, they had no future together. And what was the point of falling in love with a man she'd never see again after tonight?

Rita's heart sank when she was led onstage after Makeup. The blinding lighting and the bank of cameras reminded her she hadn't really understood how unnerving facing a live audience would be. Or facing the thousands of television watchers.

The stage was set up to look like a library. Bookshelves lined one wall. Framed pictures of past guests hung on another wall, centered around—no surprise considering the size of the man's ego—Horton's photograph.

When she stopped to blink at the lights, Horton strode to meet her and put his arm around her shoulders. "Come right on in," he said jovially as he led her to the center of the stage, where five high wooden stools waited side by side.

"I'd like to introduce you to our audience," Horton said as he beamed at her. "Why don't you start by your telling us a little about yourself and why you believe you think you're qualified to appear on our program tonight."

Taken aback, Rita stood speechless. For days, she'd been protesting her lack of qualifications for appearing on the show. Now Horton wanted to know why *she* thought she belonged here? Short of confessing the truth that she'd been suckered in by a check for five thousand dollars, she took a deep breath and gave her name and occupation.

"That's it?" Horton tried to cover his annoyance at her brief answer with an encouraging smile, but she saw the threat in his eyes. "No special qualifications to tell us about the meaning of love?"

"I'm afraid not," she answered modestly, and waited for Horton to tell *her* why she was qualified. After all, as far as she'd repeatedly told him and Eldridge, she was the last woman to sound off on subjects she knew so little about. She had two failed engagements back in Sunrise to prove it, not to mention her mistake in falling in love with a man who knew zip about love and wasn't interested in finding out! Colby had been frank enough about being attracted to her, sure, but that was about as far as he'd seemed willing to commit. Not that she really blamed him. Considering he kept using her childish nickname, in his mind she was probably still just her brothers' kid sister. On the other hand, she recalled wistfully, he hadn't kissed her as if she were.

"Come on, Rita." Horton coaxed with an eye on the closed door behind her. "I understand you work for the prominent Chicago magazine *Today's World,* which recently published Lucas Sullivan's notorious article about the six rules he believes a woman must follow to find a husband."

Rita tried to look noncommittal, but her heart was pounding madly. If the program hadn't been live, she would've turned on her heel and walked out. Discussing the meaning of love was bad enough—she'd at least expected to do that—but the thought of discussing Sullivan's Rules with Colby in front of a nationwide audience was a nightmare.

"From what I've heard," Horton went on into her silence, "Sullivan's article has set the magazine's female readers on a verbal crusade to tar and feather the man. Why don't you start by letting us hear what you think of those six highly controversial rules of Sullivan's? I'm sure there's a connection to the meaning of love, right?"

Horton turned to the audience before she had a chance to reply. "You folks must have heard about those six rules women must follow in order to find a mate, haven't you?"

Rita shifted uneasily.

The female audience broke into boos.

"So, what do you all think," Horton said, smiling into the camera. "Shall we have Ms. Rosales here give us her opinion on Sullivan's Rules?"

The audience cheered.

"I'm sorry," Rita answered with another uneasy glance at the door behind which Colby was waiting. "I'm not qualified to debate something so controversial, let alone personal."

To her dismay Horton's eyes lit up. Too late she realized that controversy was the man's middle name and the reason his program was so popular.

The audience rose to its feet and, to Rita's dismay began to chant, "Sullivan's Rules!" over and over again. Realizing the cameras were on to record her misery, Rita forced a smile. "I still can't," she repeated. "I have a highly private take on the rules and it's not for public consumption."

"But that's just what we'd like to hear," Horton said with a wink at the audience. "Right, folks?"

The audience cheered again.

Rita stopped to consider. No way could she tell anyone, let alone the audience, that she thought sexual attraction was more important in relationships than any rule of Sullivan's. Or that sex without marriage was not for her.

"Well, Ms Rosales, it looks as if we're back to the subject of the meaning of love—at least for the moment," Horton said with a tight smile. He turned his back on the audience and leaned toward Rita with narrowed eyes. "Perhaps you'd like to give back the check," he said under his breath.

For the benefit of the audience, Rita laughed as if

he'd said something that pleased her. "Don't even think about it," she whispered back. "No one messes with a Rosales from Texas."

Horton blinked and forced a laugh.

"I have someone here tonight who just might help the discussion get started." Horton finally led her to a stool and held her elbow while she squirmed her way onto a seat so high her toes didn't touch the ground.

As Rita settled onto the stool and crossed her legs, a few men in the audience whistled. It took a minute to realize her short skirt had become a lot shorter. The height of the stool was no doubt intended to give the show an extra edge by showing off feminine legs, and from the smug and satisfied look on Horton's face, it had succeeded.

He grinned at the cool look she gave him and waved to the stage manager to bring in Colby.

Her heart beating madly, Rita steeled herself to sparring with Colby on the meaning of love. Tonight, before she was through, she intended to give him a lesson or two. Maybe he'd see what he was missing.

To heck with Horton or the audience, both of which appeared to be waiting for her to make a fool of herself. If anyone was going to wind up looking a fool, it was Colby and, with luck, Horton.

Colby strode onto the set. Prompted by a stage manager off camera, the audience broke into cheers. Even as her hormones sprang to attention at the sight of the tall, lean, darn-near-perfect example of masculinity smiling at her, she tried to appear unimpressed.

"So." Horton shook hands with Colby and, with a broad wink at the audience, said, "You certainly look as if you're qualified to discuss the meaning of love with Ms. Rosales here. Do you mind telling us a little about yourself and why you volunteered to appear on our program?"

Colby gave his host the standard name, rank and serial-type bio. To Rita's avid interest, he went on to call himself a businessman dealing in imports. Rita felt relieved. The more Colby hid his real identity, the less she would have to worry about.

Surreptitiously, she studied the audience. It was thankfully smaller than she'd anticipated, and the people came in all shapes and sizes and colors. From the little she could see with the bright studio lights in her eyes, neither of the two men she'd been certain had been stalking Colby were here.

She glanced at Colby, now in casual conversation with Horton. In her private opinion Colby was taking a risk by appearing on television. *He* might not be concerned, but *she* still was.

"I understand that you and Ms. Rosales knew each other in high school and haven't seen each other since," Horton was saying. "Mind telling us how you happened to meet again and how, in your opinion, the lady has changed?"

Rita bit her lower lip to keep from interrupting. In

her book, the way Horton was speaking was insulting and patronizing. She'd fought for the right to be a strong and independent woman, she thought sourly. If she hadn't already been convinced that Horton was a true Sullivan before tonight, she was thoroughly convinced now.

She closed her eyes when Colby told the story of how they'd known each other in high school, how he'd visited her here in Chicago and surprised her. He was a darn good storyteller, Rita thought as she listened. As long as he didn't bring up her mother or, heaven forbid, launch into a description of the Texas welcome.

"...so I stopped to say hello and to deliver a message to Rita from her mother," Colby said as he ended the story. "That's about it."

Rita frowned. He had mentioned her mother. Again she thought there was more to her mother's sending Colby to give her a Texas welcome than even *he* knew.

Horton went on, "Surely you found that Ms. Rosales has changed?"

Colby's gaze swept her. "You bet," he agreed with an admiring glance at Rita. "She's become a beautiful, charming woman. Intelligent, too. As to how she feels about the meaning of love..." His voice trailed off as he grinned wickedly into Rita's blush. "She hasn't shared her thoughts with me, but I'm sure she has a number of opinions on the subject." At the intimate look Colby gave her, her heart leaped to her throat.

"Well, then, let's get started," Horton said heartily.

Horton went on to give a brief rundown to the audience on the first subject of the day: love. "I'm sure we can all agree that men and women think of love in very different ways," he said as he paced back and forth on the edge of the stage. "Right?"

The audience cheered. One man stood and shouted, "You got it!" The woman beside him pulled him down into his seat.

Rita's antennae quivered.

"Ms. Rosales is a magazine research librarian and, I understand from her bio, an avid reader." Horton turned back to Rita. "That must include reading those romantic novels, right?"

Rita nodded. A lifelong romantic, reading novels with happy endings in which a strong woman won her man and became an equal partner in a marriage was her favorite pastime. She didn't care what Horton thought, either.

"So, as a reader of romance," Horton went on with another broad wink at the audience, "you should be in a position to give us your definition of love."

Rita ignored him for a moment and turned to stare into Colby's eyes. "There are all kinds of love," she began. "The love of a mother for a child, a friend for a friend, a—"

"Come now, Ms. Rosales," Horton interjected, a smile on his lips and a frown in his eyes, "I'm sure we know all that. Right now, we're interested in the meaning of romantic love. Why don't you take a moment to think about it before you answer."

He turned to Colby. "How about you, Mr. Callahan? What's your take on love?"

Colby appeared to consider the question. "I'm not sure, but I figure love is a state of mind, a mood."

Horton perked up and turned to the audience. "A true man's answer," he said into his microphone. When the women began booing Colby and the men began to cheer, Horton turned back to Colby. "Been there, done that, have you?"

To Rita's discomfit, Colby glanced at her before he turned back to their host with a shrug. "I'm afraid not yet."

Her nerve endings tingled.

Horton checked his notes. "Your bio says you're thirty-one, Mr. Callahan. Do you expect us to believe you've never felt what you call a 'mood' for a woman?"

With Horton's question drawing Rita's attention, Colby shifted uneasily. He was as aware of his reputation back in high school as Rita was, but he'd always thought it was highly overrated. The truth about his sex life was simple. He'd been too wrapped up in his career to give much thought to a serious relationship. He'd also been too busy taking care of his mother and the foster children she kept acquiring to think seriously about male-female love.

Still, his love life was no one's business but his.

He decided to play it for laughs. "No, not really," he said with a wicked grin. "If I had, I'm sure I'd have known it."

Obviously frustrated with the lack of obtaining a cutting-edge discussion on the subject of love, Horton turned back to Rita. "What do you think of your friend's answer, Rita—you don't mind if I call you Rita, do you?"

"Of course not," Rita said agreeably, pointedly ignoring Colby. "What was the question again?"

"I believe I said that now that we have a man's viewpoint on the subject of love, what do you think of Colby's answer—from a female point of view?"

Rita stared at Colby. She didn't know about him, but she'd already learned the hard way that a woman falls in love first with her eyes, then with her mind and then with her heart. But not until Colby had reappeared in her life had she understood what it meant to fall in love with her body.

She shook her childish dreams out of her mind. This was only a television program, for heaven's sake! How could she sit here and show Colby and the viewers that her youthful infatuation for him had turned into love?

She was determined not to let him know the depth of her feelings for him. She settled for an answer that might sound corny but one that came from her heart.

"When it comes to adult love, I believe love is caring for someone more than you care for yourself. Especially in a relationship such as marriage," she said softly.

Horton frowned. "That's it?"

"Well," she added with a shrug, "take love out of a relationship and what do you have? Romantic love between two people is like being in heaven. Especially if love results in marriage and the marriage results in children."

Obviously frustrated at her less than controversial and rather old-fashioned answer, Horton stopped in his tracks. From the look on his face, she sensed he was about to come up with something that would blow the lid off her temper.

"What would the two of you think if I told you love doesn't always have much to do with relationships? What if I told you that the popular definition of love is that most people, if they're honest, actually believe men use it for sex and that women use it for marriage?"

Colby saw Rita's jaw clench and her hands ball into fists. She'd been a scrappy teenager and, unless she'd changed, it looked as if she was about to let Horton have it in front of the television cameras.

Hell, he'd seen talk shows where the contestants had erupted into a fistfight and had had to be dragged off the set. He'd even heard of a program where an irate contestant had pulled a gun and shot another contestant!

He couldn't take the chance.

Not when it was really his fault for Rita's taking part in Horton's program in the first place. He should have known she couldn't handle that much liquor. Of course, the fee she was being paid is what kept her to her agreement. He wasn't sure what Rita was going to do with her five thousand, but his was going to his mother, who was still fostering kids.

He glanced at the two empty stools, presumably there for the next segment of the program. He'd have to do something to make Horton call the interviewees out to join the discussion before Rita blew. After all, there was safety in numbers.

"Why don't we talk about something else for the moment?" Colby asked before fur could fly. When Horton hesitated, Colby slid off his stool and walked to the front of the stage. "Anyone out there who would like to join us in a debate about Sullivan's Rules?"

The audience sat in silence before it broke into applause and began to cheer.

Horton started to protest, until he saw the producer's swinging hands jabbing in the air and pointing to the audience. Obviously getting the message and recovering his cool, he joined Colby at the foot of the set. "Great idea!" he said, pounding Colby on the back. "I should have thought of it myself. Anyone out there who would like to join us onstage, raise your hand. We need one man and one woman."

When no hands were raised, Horton went on. "This is your chance to appear on television, folks. Think about it for a minute. Your five minutes of fame! Of course," he added with a glance over his shoulder at his producer, "there will be a small stipend for appearing on our program."

At the mention of a small stipend, a woman squealed and several hands shot up.

To Rita's dismay, the race to debate Sullivan's Rules was on.

Chapter Seven

With their host occupied in choosing two additional players to come up to the stage to debate Sullivan's Rules, Colby glanced over his shoulder to see Rita's reaction. Instead of looking pleased, she was perched at the edge of the stool like a bird ready to take flight.

As if she read his mind, she shot him a cool look, uncrossed her legs and tugged at her skirt.

His gaze swung to her knees. Gone were the scrawny teenage limbs with the knobby knees he remembered. Her legs were long and slender, and unless he was mistaken, her knees were dimpled.

The rest of her was interesting, too.

His forced good humor faded. If he'd hoped to turn the tables on Horton and treat the man's controversial program as a big joke, it obviously wasn't working with Rita. Since he and her brothers had always had to proceed with caution with her temper, he should have known better.

What had he been thinking when he'd encouraged her to appear on tonight's program? he asked himself. He should have known from the conversation when he'd first met the guy that he was capable of eating controversial guests like a wolf eats its hapless prey.

He shoved his hands into his pockets and turned to watch the action at the front of the stage. All while he was silently cursing his stupidity for thinking that he could drop in and out of a grown-up Rita's life without being affected. Or that what had started out as an innocent joke about giving her a message from her mother could turn into a Texas welcome that left him floored.

Worse yet, if Rita had been right about his being followed, how could he have not have realized he might put her in danger?

His next big mistake had been in not telling her that, encouraged by his Chicago Police Department counterpart, he intended to play his part on the television program as a means to hide in plain sight. Not that he didn't see *some* merit in Sullivan's Rules, though admittedly they *were* rather Victorian, but all he'd planned to do was ease the sexual tension between Rita and him. He'd sensed it building from the first moment he'd walked into her office.

Now, with two additional and unknown players involved in their debate, it looked as if he'd have to be extra careful about what he said.

He was beginning to think his mind was one card

short of a full deck as he watched the program's host play up to the audience. If he'd dreamed things would unfold as they had, he would have stayed undercover until his mission was over, then dropped in to say hello and goodbye to Rita in one short visit. He could have hightailed it back to Texas with a clear conscience.

Instead, sure as hell, he'd put himself between a rock and a hard place. He had to keep Rita reasonably placated and, at the same time, try to keep Horton from making a fool of her.

A loud and raucous audience cheered the two volunteers being escorted to the stage. Quick to take advantage of the unexpected situation, Horton greeted the female debater, a trim thirtyish blonde, with a giant hug. To Colby's amusement, the male volunteer earned merely a handshake and a slap on the shoulder.

"Well, folks, go ahead and introduce yourselves, tell us a little bit about yourselves so we can get on with the debate," Horton said to the newcomers when the audience settled down. "Before you begin, though, I want you both to make it clear to our audience that this isn't a setup. That neither of you is related to or knows Ms. Rosales or Mr. Callahan, right? You first," he said, and handed the microphone to the female volunteer.

"My name is Diane Walker," the woman said with a self-conscious giggle. "I'm from Lincoln, Nebraska. I'm a secretary visiting Chicago with my best friend. Oh, and I swear I've never met Ms. Rosales before. Or Mr. Callahan." She shot Colby an inviting glance. "I would never have forgotten meeting a guy like him." She raised her right hand and handed the microphone to the male volunteer, a husky, balding fellow with darting blue eyes.

"I'm Tim Holt from Madison, Wisconsin. I was here in Chicago for a tool-and-die convention where they handed out tickets to this program. I plan on going home tomorrow." He openly stared at Rita's knees. "I don't think I've ever met Ms. Rosales. Or Mr. Callahan."

"You sure?" Horton pretended to be incredulous.

"Yeah, I'm sure. I'd have remembered a hottie like her."

When Horton joined Holt in mentally undressing Rita, Colby's blood began to boil. From what he could recall of Sullivan's Rules, most of them were pretty personal. An intimate discussion of the mating-game relationships with Rita looking at Holt and Horton as if the pair had crawled out from under a rock was going to be a tricky matter.

He moved over to stand by Rita's stool and in an undertone, covering her microphone while he was pretending to adjust it, muttered, "Don't sweat it, Ri. No matter what Horton comes up with, I'll take care of him for you."

"No way!" Rita whispered as he managed to hide her from Horton's view for a few seconds. "I don't need you to take care of me. I've been taking care of myself for a long time!"

"Yeah," he chuckled softly as he rubbed his jaw. "I remember the time you told me to mind my own business."

Rita didn't feel sorry for having punched Colby in the jaw when she'd been too young to notice just how good-looking he was. The only girl in her family, standing up to her brothers, and Colby had been the only way to impress them with her independence. "If I ever have to, I'll do it again," she whispered back.

"Hey, all I'm asking is that you trust me," Colby said, putting the microphone back in place before he turned away.

Trust Colby? Rita shivered as his hand brushed her knee in passing. How could she trust him when she didn't know what he was up to?

When Horton motioned for a stagehand to reposition the unoccupied stools, instead of finding herself side by side with Colby, Rita found herself eyeball to eyeball with him. She opened her mouth to protest, when he held a finger to his lips.

Horton picked up the copy of the *Today's World* featuring Sullivan's Rules. He opened the magazine with an exaggerated flourish and handed it to Rita. "We'll start with you, Rita. By the way," he said to Colby, Diane and Tim, "from here on I'll call you by your first names. We like things a little less formal around here, okay?"

After a smirk at the audience, and without waiting for an answer, Horton went on. "Rita, how about reading Sullivan's rule number one to the audience?"

Rita took a deep breath to calm herself and plunged right in. She'd gone this far and there was no turning back.

"'A happy relationship requires that a woman make her man feel masculine.'"

Horton nodded solemnly. "Right on," he agreed solemnly. "That's a very important rule. What do you think about it, Rita?"

With Colby gazing at her wryly, Rita decided to tell it as she saw it. Besides, if the question about making a man feel masculine included Colby, he was masculine enough for two men. "Actually," she said with a cool glance into Colby's eyes, "I think it's more a question of a woman having to feed a man's ego than trying to make him feel masculine."

"And what's your opinion about this rule, Diane?" Horton prompted as the audience burst into boisterous laughter.

She giggled. "I don't really know that much about a man's ego, but the truth is, I'm for whatever it takes to get a man interested in me."

Tim, seated beside Colby, raised his clasped hands and shook them over his head in a silent salute.

The women in the audience cheered.

"Really! In that case," Horton said with a fake

frown, "I guess you don't believe in Sullivan's second rule for the mating game, either."

Diane frowned uneasily. "Do you mind telling me what it is?"

"Hold on a minute and I'll read it to you."

Horton took back the magazine from Rita and began to read aloud.

"'While a man is not monogamous by nature, he is more likely to see a woman as a potential girlfriend or mate if sexual intimacy doesn't occur too soon.'

"Or," Horton went on as Diane gasped, "the next rule—'A woman must rein in her own desires to promote the health of the relationship.'"

Diane shook her head. "That doesn't sound right. Are you sure that's what Sullivan said?"

"Absolutely." Horton handed her the open magazine. "You don't agree?"

"No, I don't," Diane said as she glanced at Sullivan's article and passed the magazine back to Horton. "If you ask me, the guy who wrote it is dead wrong. What's a relationship without sex?"

"Right!" Horton said gleefully.

Tim guffawed. "That's for damn sure!"

Men in the audience began to hoot.

Wisely, Colby remained silent.

Rita shifted on the stool and glared at Horton with fire in her eyes. "Sex isn't a game!" she blurted. "There has to be a deeper meaning in a relationship or sex is just another activity."

Horton looked pleased. "I can see you have an opinion on the subject, Rita. Colby? How about sharing your opinion with us?"

It took all of Colby's control to keep from punching the smirk off Horton's face. Instead, he forced himself to give the controversial answer Horton expected. After all, that was what he'd been paid for.

"It sounds as if Sullivan's gotten pretty close, but maybe not close enough. I've heard a real and lasting relationship isn't possible if bells don't start to ring when you hear a person's voice."

When Colby's gaze locked with hers, Rita felt a warm glow around her heart. In spite of what she'd believed about Colby's chauvinistic leanings, his take on Sullivan's rules for the mating game seemed to be close to her own. Maybe there was hope for him yet.

Horton nodded thoughtfully. "So, Colby, from what you've told us in our earlier discussion of the meaning of love, I take it you haven't yet been in what you call a 'mood' to hear those bells ringing?"

"Like I said before, I can't be sure," Colby said as he reluctantly tore his gaze away from Rita. It wasn't easy to ignore her intent eyes, not when he could've sworn he was hearing bells. "From what I've learned from the examples of my closest male friends, lasting relationships seem to happen only after a long courtship. As for me, I've never had the time."

"So," Horton went on, "even if you've never entertained the idea of a sexual relationship, I take it you're a believer in the Sullivan rule that says in order to get her man a woman must strive for compatibility rather than trying to be sexy?"

Colby shrugged. "I suppose you could put it that way."

Rita's looked at him speculatively. *There was indeed hope for Colby.*

Tim snorted.

Diane's expression turned to one of horror. "You mean, no sex?"

The audience started shouting protests against platonic relationships.

Horton beamed.

Colby realized the show's host had finally gotten what he'd been waiting for, a cutting-edge discussion of Sullivan's Rules. At the rate things were going downhill, Horton had to be pleased with him, but as far as Rita was concerned, it looked as if he was dead meat.

Horton jumped in before the noise died down. "And how about the Sullivan rule that a woman must show her man how much she likes and appreciates him?"

He went on before Colby could reply. "Sullivan also says a woman must treat her man with affection and sublimate her own daily frustrations," he added with a smirk. "Let's hear from you this time, Tim."

"As long as it includes letting the man make out, and I do mean make out, that rule sounds okay to me!" Tim shouted.

Diane leaped in. "I'm not about to do what that says—sublimate any of my frustrations! A woman has the same right to initiate sex as a man!"

"Nah! Personally," Tim said with a leer, "I think us guys ought to treat Sullivan to a beer for coming up with rules like that."

The men in the audience stood up and cheered. More than one woman poked her male partner with her elbow.

Rita stole a glance at her watch while the argument continued. If the show kept up like this, someone was going to get hurt. Thank goodness there were only ten more minutes to go before the program was over and she could tell Horton just what she thought of him, his program and his tactics.

As for Sullivan's rules for the mating game, she planned to tell Horton that Lucas Sullivan, April Morgan's new husband, might have written those rules, but that Lucas now knew better. She intended to point out that marriage to April had sent Sullivan back for additional research.

As for Colby— well, he'd almost redeemed himself with his comment about bells ringing when the ideal mate came along. Almost, but not quite.

She turned her attention away from Colby to what was happening onstage. There was still Sullivan's rule number six to debate, and Horton seemed to have forgotten about it. She raised her hand and reminded him.

"Oh, by all means," Horton replied. "Yes, indeed, rule six is one that's close to *my* heart." He handed the magazine to Colby. "Why don't you read it to the audience."

"'A woman must be supportive,'" Colby read, "'fun-loving, easygoing and generous in her praise of a man's achievements.' Wow. Quite a rule."

"Quite a rule?" Rita said, outraged. "Anyone who believes that rule is a jerk. That kind of behavior has to be a two-way street. The mating game isn't only about what men want. Women have needs, too."

"I agree with you, but it's not that important," Diane said. "Personally, I like the sex part of the rules better. Besides, married or not," she said with a coy glance at Tim Holt, "I sure don't intend to grow old alone."

Rita felt oddly pleased that the blonde had apparently decided to target Holt instead of Colby.

"Thank you for those words, Diane—I think many in our audience would agree," Horton said jovially. "As for Sullivan's Rules, it looks as if we did find out something about the mating game tonight. Opinion seems to be that while Sullivan is more right than wrong, everyone's entitled to make up his or her own rules in the mating game."

He smiled benevolently at Rita and Colby before he added slyly, "Sometimes rules work and sometimes they don't, but when a couple's destined for each other, well, hang the rules! That's it for tonight, folks."

When background music sounded, Horton waved to the audience. "See you next week when we'll have another interesting subject to share."

The music swelled. At a signal, the audience cheered. In seconds, the program was over.

Horton rushed up. Before Colby and Rita could move, Horton grasped their hands and beamed at them. "You two were great! The sparks between the two of you! Say, how would you like to come back? We can discuss sexual attraction versus natural selection."

"Not on your life!" Rita said without hesitation. He'd managed to pick the one subject that she preached but couldn't bring herself to practice. She cast a glance at Colby. His gaze seemed to be following Diane as the woman sashayed off the stage, clinging to Tim Holt's arm. The one man she was truly attracted to was not only interested but unreliable.

When she did decide to join the mating game, it was going to be with a man who made her feel safe before she fell asleep at night and made her feel happy when she woke up. As a lawman who kept reappearing and disappearing without notice, Colby didn't come close.

Horton grinned. "I like the way your faces give you away when you get all riled up. The audience seems to have picked up on your reactions, too. Why don't you both take some time to think about my offer? If it'll help you decide, the fee will be the same each time the two of you appear." His gaze settled on Rita. "If you agree, it might even be pumped up a notch."

Colby grabbed Rita by an elbow before she could take a swing at their grinning host. "Thanks just the same," he said as he drew her off the set. "Rita's much too busy. Besides, like I said, I'm going back to Texas."

Without waiting for Horton to continue his campaign to change their minds, Colby led Rita offstage and out into the cool night air.

"How about I take you out for a late dinner?" he said when he came to a stop beside her car in the parking lot. "You claimed Melvin's Diner was one of your favorite restaurants, but you didn't eat much this afternoon."

Rita shook her head. Her stomach still felt queasy. "Thanks, but I don't think I could eat a bite."

Colby looked disappointed. "I was hoping the night air would make you feel better. If you aren't hungry, how about a cup of coffee?"

"No," she said. "If you don't mind, I think I'd rather just go home."

"You're sure?" Colby coaxed. "I'd hate to think this is going to be the last time we see each other."

Rita managed a shrug, but she couldn't agree with him more. The thought of never seeing him again left her feeling hollow. Nevertheless she said, "I'm not sure what brought you here to Chicago, but I'm sure we'll run into each other again someday."

"Someday? Why not now?"

Her resistance was crumbling, but she said, "Why can't we just say good night right here?"

"Because there are too many people around, for one thing." Horton's audience was pouring into the parking lot. "For another—" instead of shaking her hand, he ran his fingers over it, then her wrist "—I'd really like to make this a proper Texas good night."

Rita shivered and it wasn't because of the cool air. She knew all there was to know about a Texas welcome, but a Texas good-night?

She had a feeling it wasn't like any good-night she'd ever experienced. She wasn't sure she was quite ready for it.

Unfortunately, there was a problem. His warm fingers on her wrist were sending electric shocks through her, breaking down her emotional barriers. "You mean goodbye, not good night, don't you?"

"No." The gaze Colby locked with hers was intense. "I've just realized that my plan to take you out for dinner wasn't meant to be goodbye. In fact, I'm not ready to say goodbye. Not yet."

Rita didn't know if she was right in reading Colby's intentions, but it suddenly felt as if butterflies had found a home in her stomach. "You're not?"

"No, I'm not." He stared at her as if he were seeing her for the first time. "If you don't want dinner, how about if we go somewhere quiet so we can make this a proper good night?"

Her hand enfolded in Colby's, Rita realized she wasn't ready to say goodbye, either.

"Okay," she said.

It was beginning to look as if she'd been right when she'd talked about the importance of sexual attraction. Falling in love might not have a rational basis, in spite of Sullivan's Rules. If it had, she would have sent Colby packing by now. Not say what she was about to.

"I'd feel a lot better saying good night at my place. It's not very far. Besides, it's a heck of a lot safer. There can't possibly be anyone living in my building who could be out to get you. Or anyone around to frighten the life out of me, either."

Colby laughed and squeezed her hand. "Still a victim of your imagination, I see. If it'll make you feel any better, I've got Chicago's finest on my side. Let's go. I no longer have the rental car—took a cab here today. Do you have a car?"

"Yes, let's go," she murmured. She took her car keys from her bag, thinking if she had any common sense left after seeing Colby again and discovering how much she cared about him, she'd drop him at his hotel, say good-night and go home to bed. Alone.

Even as she tried to rationalize what might come next if she wasn't careful, she crossed to her car with Colby and motioned for him to get in on the passenger side.

He slid in beside her, close enough for her to feel

the warmth of his body, to be aware of the faint scent of his shaving lotion.

Close enough for her to shiver in anticipation of the possibilities the evening held….

Chapter Eight

"Nice place you have here." Colby trailed Rita into her tiny apartment and paused to admire it. "Although I have to say it doesn't look like you."

"You mean it doesn't look like the person I used to be," Rita said, looking around at her eclectic furnishings. "It's not only the furnishings that are different, or haven't you noticed?"

"I've noticed." Colby's frankly admiring gaze swung to her. His eyes twinkled, and a smile curved his lips. "You're nothing like the girl I once knew. No, that's not right. You *are* like her, only a hundred times better."

Rita blushed. He was right about her no longer being the girl, a tomboy really, she once was, she thought as she kicked off her shoes and shed her jacket. And the furnishings of the apartment were just another way to show him just how much she *had* changed.

As the youngest, and unexpected, child in a family with four boys, her bedroom at home had been furnished by a mother determined to turn the tomboy into a girl. Chintz and maple and stuffed animals. She shuddered.

Instead of being pleased with her mother's attention, Rita remembered yearning for the same freedom her parents afforded her brothers and the boy who lived next door, Colby. The boys' behavior had always been regarded with an amused "boys will be boys" attitude, while her boyish behavior had been regarded as somewhat inappropriate.

Her furniture now was sleek and Swedish. Instead of a four-poster bed, a simple couch opened into a bed at night. The coffee table, if required, could be raised to become a small dining table. A comfortable upholstered armchair, two chairs and a small television and a few lamps completed the furnishings. The effect was clean and lean, and much to Rita's satisfaction.

"I like your Christmas tree." Colby leaned over to smell the fresh pine scent of the little tree she'd brought home last week and been too busy to decorate. "Need any help decorating it?"

"Not really." Rita laughed. "The tree is so small it won't take me but a few minutes to trim it. I've just been too busy. Would you like coffee?"

"Mind if I make myself comfortable first?"

Uneasy, Rita wondered just how comfortable Colby intended to make himself. She soon found out. He took off his jacket and tie, unbuttoned the two top buttons of his shirt and rolled up his sleeves.

While he'd filled out a little, the past ten years hadn't done much to change his lean muscular build. He was still tall with broad shoulders and a tapered waist. His hands were large, his fingers long and graceful. His brown hair, except for the unruly cowlick that kept falling over his eyes, was streaked with Texas sunshine.

He'd been the most handsome boy she'd ever met. Now he was the most handsome man.

She began to doubt the wisdom of putting herself alone with Colby and her waltzing hormones. She moved into the kitchen. "I'll have coffee ready in a few minutes!"

Colby followed her into the tiny kitchen. "Need any help?"

Colby standing behind her, his breath warming the back of her neck, Rita thought of lots of things they could do together. She felt suddenly afraid. Afraid of the possibilities her small studio apartment afforded. Things were moving too fast.

"Thanks, but no thanks," she said with an apologetic smile, and rubbed her shoulder where she'd bumped it against a hanging shelf. "I'm afraid there's not enough room for two in here. You're bound to get hurt, too."

"Sorry about that," he said. "Would it help if I massaged your shoulder? I can make the hurt go away."

Rita thought of his offer for all of two seconds. A massage? Not if he had to stand closer to her than he was now. "No, thanks, I'll be fine in a minute."

Colby backed out of the kitchen, but not before he reached over Rita's shoulder for an open tin of cookies she'd left on the counter.

He sniffed at the cookies and broke into a wide smile. "Your mother's?"

Rita smiled. "Mom sends me a care package almost every week. I think she's convinced I'll become skin and bones without her baking."

Colby eyed her approvingly. "When I pass through Sunrise again, I'll be sure to tell your mother you're holding up nicely. Very nicely. Uh, you don't mind if I try a few cookies while I wait for the coffee, do you?"

"Help yourself," Rita said, remembering how Colby and her brothers had always been unabashed in their addiction to her mother's baked goods.

Munching a cookie, Colby wandered back to the living room and the large picture window. Although not on the lake, the building was situated in such a way that Lake Michigan could be glimpsed between the trees and buildings. There was also a wide expanse of star-studded sky. "Nice view," he said over his shoulder. "Your rent must be high. No wonder you were willing to appear on Horton's program."

Having put the coffeepot on, Rita emerged from the kitchen. "You're right about that. I also need the

The Harlequin Reader Service® — Here's how it works:

If offer card is missing write to: Harlequin Reader Service, 3010 Walden Ave., P.O. Box 1867, Buffalo NY 14240-1867

NO POSTAGE
NECESSARY
IF MAILED
IN THE
UNITED STATES

BUSINESS REPLY MAIL
FIRST-CLASS MAIL   PERMIT NO. 717-003   BUFFALO, NY

POSTAGE WILL BE PAID BY ADDRESSEE

HARLEQUIN READER SERVICE
3010 WALDEN AVE
PO BOX 1867
BUFFALO NY 14240-9952

Play the

Lucky Hearts Game

and get...

2 FREE BOOKS

and a FREE MYSTERY GIFT...

YES! YOURS to KEEP!

I have scratched off the silver card. Please send me my 2 FREE BOOKS and FREE mystery GIFT. I understand that I am under no obligation to purchase any books as explained on the back of this card.

Scratch Here!

then look below to see what your cards get you... 2 Free Books & a Free Mystery Gift!

354 HDL D34Z   154 HDL D35K

FIRST NAME

LAST NAME

ADDRESS

APT.#

CITY

STATE/PROV.

ZIP/POSTAL CODE

(H-AR-12/04)

Twenty-one gets you
2 FREE BOOKS
and a **FREE MYSTERY GIFT!**

Twenty gets you
2 FREE BOOKS!

Nineteen gets you
1 FREE BOOK!

TRY AGAIN!

money to see me through the holiday season." She crossed to stand beside him at the window. "I like to look out the window at the lake and sky," she said. "If the weather's right, I make great cloud pictures."

Colby turned to study her. "Cloud pictures? I thought only kids did that."

"Not only kids, people with imagination, too—which you know I have." She laughed. "You ought to see the clouds in the spring. The fluffy white ones look like big sheep on the run." Rita threw open her hands to demonstrate.

Watching her demonstrate cloud pictures, Colby became fascinated with the change he saw in her. The grown-up Rita had some of the same endearing qualities she'd shown as a girl when she hadn't been pestering him and her brothers to include her in their rough-and-tumble games. "What do you do in the winter?"

She laughed again. "In the winter, the clouds produce snow, and sometimes I build a snowman in the front yard, carrot for a nose and all."

"Now, that sounds like the old Rita I remember," Colby said as he covertly admired the way her spirited gestures had pulled her blouse taut over her breasts. He took a deep breath. She might have sounded like the old Rita, but she sure didn't look like her.

Rita frowned. "Is that bad?"

"No, not at all." Colby put any sensual thoughts on the back burner—for the moment. He changed the subject. "Now that there's no Horton around to hear the truth, did you really mean what you said about the meaning of love? That it's about caring for someone more than you care for yourself, and romantic love is like being in heaven?"

Rita thought about the way she'd carried on to cover up the uncertainty she felt on the subject of love.

"To be honest," she said with an embarrassed smile, "I just said the first thing that came into my mind."

"Oh? Does that mean you've never been in love?"

She paused, startled, her gaze on the lake beyond. Unbidden memories of Colby in high school surfaced. For sure, she'd had a crush on Colby then, maybe what some called puppy love, but real adult love? "No, I don't think so. Why?"

Colby shrugged. "No reason. I just remembered your mother mentioned you'd been engaged to be married but called the wedding off."

"That's true," Rita agreed. "As a matter of fact, twice. Almost three times."

He stared at her. "You're kidding. Anyone I know?"

"Maybe. The first time was to Raul Garcia, a family friend my folks kept pushing on me. Stupidly, I let myself be convinced it was the right thing to do. Until I realized Dad wanted me to marry Raul because he thought I needed someone older and wiser to look after me. As if I couldn't take care of myself!"

Colby nodded. "So what about the second time?"

Rita grimaced. "After my father got through lecturing me on my lack of responsibility, in a moment of rebellion I turned to Buddy Hansen. He was in my class at college and I figured he was young enough to understand how I felt. I also wanted my parents to see that I could do my own choosing. It only took Buddy and me a week to realize we'd made a mistake getting engaged. We broke it off."

"Chalk another one up for you," Colby said admiringly. "And the third guy?"

Rita smiled ruefully at the memory of Bill Langston, the lawyer her mother had set her up with next. A pleasant man, he was not the least bit interested in someone as young as Rita. He did offer his services as her lawyer if she ever needed one, she told Colby. "Actually, we parted friends. I still get cards from him and his wife at Christmas."

Rita turned to face Colby. "How about you?" she asked. "It's hard to believe that a guy like you hasn't met a woman you cared for enough to marry sometime during the last ten years."

Colby popped the last bite of his cookie into his mouth, chewed slowly, then dusted the crumbs off his chin. "I'm not sure what you mean by 'a guy like me,' but what with college, joining the Rangers and trying to keep an eye on my mother's foster children, the truth is I've been too busy. As for finding a woman I really liked—" He stopped abruptly. A surprised look came over his face as he stared at her. "Not until now."

Startled at the idea that she could be the woman Colby fell in love with, Rita did the only thing she could think of. She ran into the kitchen. "Coffee must be ready by now," she explained. Colby remained where he was.

Maybe she hadn't heard him right. Maybe she'd heard what she wanted to hear. But any way she looked at the astonishing notion, Colby seemed equally uncertain about what he'd just said. He was probably too embarrassed to confront her in the kitchen or he was having second thoughts.

For a guy who'd always been confident to the point of arrogance, Colby was an enigma.

In any case, it looked as if she'd inadvertently managed to take another giant step in making Colby think of her as a grown woman. She filled two cups with the steaming hazelnut-flavored coffee, left his black and added cream to hers, placed them on a tray with some of her mother's cookies and took the tray out to the living room. Colby was still standing, gazing out the window. He turned when he heard her set the tray on the coffee table.

"What did you mean when you told Horton love is merely a mood?" she asked him, straightening. "No, forget that. What you told Horton doesn't matter. More to the point—" she took a deep breath "—what did you mean by 'not until now'?"

"Beats me," he muttered, and started toward the door. "The coffee smells great, but having expressed that stupid opinion, maybe I ought to say goodbye and leave before I make a complete ass of myself."

That didn't sound like him, Rita thought with a frown. Still, she didn't intend to give up now. "Inventing off-the-cuff answers to a question about the meaning of love in front of television cameras is one thing. Telling the truth is another." She felt emboldened. "Now that we're alone, and before you disappear, what did you mean by that 'not until now'?"

Colby turned to face her, and he looked quite taken aback. "First of all, I *didn't* mean to say goodbye the other night. Since I was toying with the idea of hanging around Chicago for a while, I really only meant good night." He shrugged. "So, would it help if I apologized?"

Rita thought fast. He still hadn't answered her question, but in asking Colby up for coffee tonight, she'd not only wanted to show him she was no longer the girl back home, she'd planned to experiment with her intention to remain a virgin until she was married.

It might be the wrong time, the wrong place and the wrong man, but the truth was, he knew her well enough to figure out that he'd managed to awaken a vulnerable chord in her. He had to know she was attracted to him.

She thought back to their television appearance,

to a moment when a surprised look had come over Colby's face as he'd blithely said he'd have to hear bells ring in order to know when the right woman came along.

Had he heard bells?

Was he hearing them now?

Was that what he'd meant by "not until now"?

Gazing at him, she realized he had indeed recognized her as a woman. Now the question seemed to be: was she still determined to remain a virgin?

As if in a dream, she found herself ignoring the fragrant coffee she'd set out. She moved closer to Colby. He lifted his arms and draped them loosely over her shoulders.

Colby's cautious body language, his hesitancy in explaining the "not until now" comment, told her that the next move was up to her. Wordlessly, she put her arms around his neck and pulled his head down to hers.

"Ri?"

"No, Rita," she said softly. "You said 'not until now' a moment ago. Tell me what you meant."

Colby held her away from him. "I think you know."

"Do I?" she whispered.

He pulled her close and spoke into her neck. "I must sound like a fool, but until now I've never had a reason to think about you like this. I'm afraid the kid back home kept getting in the way."

She turned her head and kissed his chin. "Go on, you're doing great."

"The crazy truth is," Colby obliged, his eyes on hers now, "I've had the strangest feeling from the moment I walked through your office door the other day and you looked up at me. It's taken a few days for me to get used to it. The feeling, I mean."

He shook his head. "I knew you'd grown into quite a beauty. Your mother told me how beautiful you were whenever I dropped in on my way to and from Waco. And the photograph of you at your friend's wedding confirmed it. But the sheer physical reality of you, the intelligence in those green eyes…"

He brought his mouth to hers and kissed her till her toes curled. But in some part of her mind, a nagging voice questioned the wisdom of giving herself to a man who had not yet said he loved her. She was also concerned about the silly photograph. *Was* there a connection between having caught the bridal bouquet and Colby's appearance? It was starting to seem that way.

She pulled back her head, ending the kiss. Colby only chuckled at the worried expression she knew must be on her face and lowered his mouth to hers for another kiss, then another, trying to fulfill his new awareness of her. "This is crazy, no?" he said when he came up for air.

"This is crazy, yes," she murmured in reply, helpless now to resist him. She'd never experienced anything like this. Twenty-eight years was long enough to wait for the sexual experience she'd been preaching about. "Kiss me again, please."

After realizing that her oft-repeated theory— that sexual compatibility had to be number one on the list of reasons for entering a lasting relationship—was actually true, Rita lost herself in Colby's kiss. She no longer felt any doubt that sexual attraction was the actual basis for developing a real and lasting relationship.

As for Sullivan's recommendation that the mating game required a long courtship, well, that was okay with her—just as long as the man courting her was the man now holding her in his arms.

She didn't need an experiment to prove it, either.

The telephone rang before she could tell Colby so.

"Don't answer that," Colby said, holding her still when she tried to turn away. "Whoever's calling can leave a message."

"No, I wish I could, but I can't. It has to be my mother. She usually calls once a week." Rita smiled ruefully and pulled out of Colby's arms. "It may sound crazy, but Mom says she has to know I'm okay. Smother love is one reason I moved to Chicago."

Colby let her go, but very reluctantly. His finely honed sixth sense warned him Rita's mood was about to change. And not for the better.

She motioned to him to wait while she picked up the phone. "Hi, Mom. Of course I knew it was you. Who else calls me so late? Yes, I know it's an hour earlier in Texas. And yes, I'm fine. Yes, I got your latest package. The cookies are great."

Watching Colby, she listened as her mother went on. "Yes, Colby's here. How did you know?" Her eyes narrowed. "You sent him?" Still watching Colby, she listened to a long explanation. "Yes, I'm sure he's doing what you told him to do. I've got to go now, Mom. I'll call you back tomorrow. Give Dad a hug for me. Yes, I'll tell Colby you said hello. 'Night."

Rita hung up, folded her arms across her chest and stared at Colby.

"Everything okay?"

"That depends on your point of view," she said. It was clear to her now that sending Colby to visit her was a setup. Her mother did indeed see him as a future son-in-law. It wasn't Colby's fault, but right now she felt so manipulated, so treated like a child, whether or not Colby was complicit in her mother's plan, that all she wanted was to be left alone.

When Colby moved to take her in his arms again, Rita stepped back.

"It's that darn photograph, I know it is," she muttered. "You can go home and tell her I'm single and I intend to stay that way."

"That's a pity," Colby murmured, again trying to pull her into his embrace. "I love the little crinkles that appear at the sides of your eyes when you frown."

She struggled out of his arms and took a deep breath. "Don't try to change the subject. When I decide to get married, it won't be because my mother approves. Furthermore, if all you came up here for was a cup of coffee—and maybe a seduction—you're not going to get either one."

"Hold on a minute!" Colby interjected, frustrated as hell. "You and I know this argument isn't about a cup of coffee. If you're angry with your mother, don't take it out on me. I was just trying to do your mother a favor. That is, before…" He gestured helplessly.

"I don't care! There's a coffee shop still open down the street. Maybe you ought to go there now before they close." She strode to the tiny kitchen, grabbed the tin of her mother's cookies and thrust it into his hands. "Since you like these so much, you can take them with you."

"I'm sorry about this, Ri," Colby said, filled with regret for a night that had held so much promise and was ending so miserably. "Forget your mother. This is about you and me. No matter what you believe, I think I do care about you."

"You *think?* When do you *think* you'd know? Before or after we made love?"

Colby raked his hair off his forehead. "The truth is, I'm on a special assignment here in Chicago. An assignment that may get ugly. I don't want to involve you."

"Involve me? Considering that every time you and

I have been together someone's been out to get you, your concern for me is a little late."

Colby had to admit that Rita was right. Originally, he hadn't intended to do more than drop in to say hello and goodbye. The trouble had started because he'd been so intrigued by the grown-up Rita that he hadn't been able to leave without seeing her again. No matter how he'd justified appearing in public with her, in hindsight his decision had been stupid.

Maybe it wasn't too late to make amends.

"It still could be a case of your overactive imagination, you know. But before you say anything, I'm not going to take a chance by hanging around you. There's an old Texas Ranger rule that cautions not to get emotionally involved with anyone while on an assignment, so—"

"It was not my imagination!" Rita interrupted. "I'm not only sure there are people following you, I'm convinced *you're* the one who needs someone to watch your back!"

"Like you?"

"If that's what it takes, yes."

Colby smothered a grin. It was the old Rita, I-can-do-anything-you-can-do talking. The last thing he wanted was to feed Rita's temper. "Come on, Ri. If you're right, the people I'm involved with could eat you for breakfast if they wanted to. Let's face it, you're the last person to take on the role of a bodyguard."

"The name is Rita and I've done okay as your bodyguard so far," Rita said belligerently.

This was no time to tell her that she was the last person he'd choose to be his bodyguard. Not when she turned men's heads. "It still could be your imagination." He delivered his words with a laugh, attempting to lighten the situation.

Rita marched to the door and held it open. "Since this all seems like a big joke to you, out!"

Colby gave in and moved to the door. "You really want me to leave without saying a proper good night?"

"I do. And while we're on the subject, let me tell you something. You can go home and tell my mother the wedding-bouquet superstition skipped me. If and when I do decide to get married, no one's going to choose the man but me."

Colby held up his hands in surrender. "Have it your way. But in case something comes up and you need me in the next few days, you can leave a message for me at Chicago Police Department headquarters."

"No way! And, furthermore, when you do see my mother, you can tell her all you were able to talk me out of were her cookies."

"Oh, I don't know…" Colby lingered with a teasing smile. "You sure know how to kiss."

Fuming, Rita pointed to the door.

Colby heaved a sigh. "If that's the way you really

feel, I'll leave. But not before I give you that proper good night I promised you."

Before Rita had a chance to tell Colby she wasn't interested in any more "proper good-nights," he pulled her into his arms and smiled down into her eyes. "Ready?"

Outraged, Rita opened her mouth to say no.

"Isn't this better than fighting?" Colby murmured as he brought his face closer to hers.

This, to Rita's dismay, was to hold her head between his two hands, smile into her widened eyes and gently brush his thumbs over her cheeks. "Your skin feels like satin," he said softly. "Where have you been hiding all these years? How could I not have known—" Rita's nerves quivered with excitement "—or at least guessed there was a desirable woman hiding under that tomboy facade of yours?" He sighed. "But we could still be friends."

At last he pulled away.

He hadn't actually kissed her.

"I'm afraid I'd better go while I'm still in my right mind," Colby said while Rita just gazed at him, dumbfounded. "What made me think we could only be friends when friendship seems to be the last thing on my mind?"

With a final touch of a fingertip to her cheek, he turned and left.

When she was able to move again, Rita stepped forward and closed the door behind him. She'd managed to teach him she wasn't the tomboy he'd known in Texas, but in the process it seemed that she'd learned a lesson of her own:

If she'd been saving herself for the ultimate sexual experience of the marriage bed with the right man, she knew now that Colby could have been that man.

And that maybe now he never would be.

Chapter Nine

After spending a sleepless night curled on the couch trying to forget Colby—she hadn't even bothered to open the couch into a bed—Rita arrived at the office the next morning an hour late. She encountered Arthur wheeling his refreshment cart out of her office.

"Hi, Rita! Guess I'm not the only one around here with a significant other," he said with a knowing grin.

Rita had to smile. Ever since she'd introduced Arthur to a co-worker who had lately become his fiancée, Arthur wanted to see everyone in a happy romantic relationship. "What makes you say so?" she asked.

"I just left a gift on your desk for you," he said. "If you ask me, it's something *very* special."

Well, she thought, whatever he'd left for her had made his day. A look over his shoulder told her why. A long white florist box tied with a red ribbon lay in the middle of her desk.

She stepped into the office and eyed the box dubiously. "Are you sure this is for me?"

Arthur abandoned his beverage cart in the hall and trailed her into her office. "Yeah, I'm sure," he said, beaming. "Your name is on the outside of the gift envelope."

Rita reached for the small envelope tucked into the ribbon and drew out a small card. "All this says is 'Good night.'"

Arthur's smile turned anxious. "Good night? It's only ten o'clock in the morning. Are you sure?"

"Don't ask," Rita said as she untied the ribbon and opened the box. The red roses could only have been sent by Colby as an apology for last night. If so, they held a world of meaning too precious to share with anyone. Lost in thought, she motioned to the door. "Thanks for bringing these up, Arthur."

"I'll be back with fresh coffee in a minute, okay?" Arthur said, obviously reluctant to leave without finding out who had sent the flowers.

At the mention of coffee, the image of Colby, the man she'd spent the night trying to forget, suddenly became bigger than life. The roses told her that one way or another she hadn't heard the last of him. "No, thanks. Maybe later," Rita murmured.

She waited until Arthur left before she lifted the ten beautiful roses nested in a cocoon of green tissue paper out of the florist box. Why ten, she wasn't sure, but she knew that red roses were for passion.

They had to be a reminder of the final good-night kiss Colby had planned but didn't deliver.

Or, she finally realized as she gazed at the roses, there was one rose for each year since she'd last seen him.

A delicious excitement filled her at the memory of the way Colby had kissed her before her mother had called. The boy she'd grown up with, of all people!

She'd already known that under his six feet two of raw masculinity Colby was a man of many talents, but, looking at the lovely roses, the last thing she'd expected was that he was also a romantic. For only a romantic could have thought of a message so simple and so deep with meaning. A message only the two of them would have understood.

If the roses were an apology for kissing her or *not* kissing her, Colby had nothing to apologize for. She'd been the seducer. She'd been the one who had lost her temper. She'd been the one to call a halt to the romantic interlude and send him away. No wonder he hadn't tried to kiss her before he left.

Rita sighed. Maybe she was reading more into last night than she should. Colby had made no secret of his passion for law enforcement and that he intended to return to Texas.

She buried her nose in the roses, inhaling their delicious fragrance. She was ready to admit that if anyone needed to apologize for the way last night had ended, it wasn't Colby. It was she.

"Rita Rosales! How could you without telling us?"

Us turned out to be her friends April and Lili,

who'd come into her office and were avidly eyeing the box of roses.

"Tell you what?" As if she didn't know, Rita thought wryly. She knew that news traveled faster than lightning at a small magazine like *Today's World.* "I guess Arthur didn't waste any time spreading the word, but it's no use. I don't know for sure who sent the roses."

"For sure?" April echoed. "That means you must know something. Give!"

"I *think* they're a gift from Colby Callahan," Rita said, unwilling to share the whole truth behind the gift. "I'm not a hundred percent certain."

"Arthur's not the only one who's talking," April said as she studied the roses. "The mail-room staff is taking bets on the sender."

"No way! Who are they betting on?"

"So far, Tom Eldridge seems to be the odds-on favorite."

Rita laughed. "Tom's not the type to send roses. He's the least likely person to be romantic around here. Lili can testify to that."

Lili blushed.

"Oh, I don't know." April leaned over to smell the roses. "The rumor is Tom's grateful to you for last night's debate on Paul Horton's show."

April's eyes narrowed when she noticed the small envelope and card on Rita's desk. "A floral delivery doesn't happen every day around here," she said. "So why don't you give us the who, why and what happened between you and Colby. That should help explain the roses. I watched the two of you on Horton's show last night, and the sparks were flying like fireworks on the Fourth of July. Anyone could have noticed it. But I guess that's the problem. Why would Colby send you roses after the way the two of you went at it?" She paused and peered at Rita over her glasses. "You two didn't happen to get together after the program, did you?"

Rita gave up her pretense of innocence. Her friends knew her too well. She nodded reluctantly. "We did."

She got up, took a vase off a shelf behind her desk and gently, one by one, placed the roses into it. "I'll have to get some water," she murmured. "Anyway, what we did, or rather what we didn't do, isn't what you're thinking. All that happened was that I invited Colby to my apartment for coffee. And before the two of you get any wrong ideas," she added when April's mouth fell open, "one of the reasons I invited him up was because I wanted to show him I wasn't the kid from back home anymore."

Lili's eyes glowed with admiration. "You are so brave," she sighed. "I wish I knew how to show Tom Eldridge how I feel about him."

April shot Lili a sympathetic look. "I have a feeling you'll be able to attract his attention soon. Now that I've taken care of educating Lucas, I'm going to help you." She turned back to Rita. "Go on, Rita."

"The other reason I invited Colby to my apartment," Rita said, "was because I'd realized that whenever he's out in the open, he appears to be someone's target. So I wanted him safe in my place."

Lili shivered. "Oh, my! A man of danger!"

Rita went on to tell April and Lili about what had happened at La Paloma and Melvin's Diner. "I tried to warn Colby, but the man just doesn't want to believe me. He keeps insisting it's only my imagination working overtime."

"Men like to think they're smarter than women, but don't stop there," April said with a grin. "What happened next?"

Rita's blood sizzled as she relived the moments with Colby before her mother's telephone call broke the spell. "I guess you could say one thing almost led to another."

April chortled. "That's another way of saying you almost had sex. And then what?"

"And then nothing." Rita frowned at the memory of how upset she'd been after she'd learned that her mother had hoped she and Colby would become an item after he dropped in to see her. "That's when my mother called."

Lili whispered. "No! While you were embracing?"

"Well, yes," Rita said with a blush, "but we were only kissing. When my mother asked if Colby was there, I had to say yes. After all, I was practically in his lap. I'm afraid I blew up when Mom asked me if

Colby was doing what she'd sent him to do. That did it! Up until then I'd thought the whole scenario was great spontaneous combustion."

"Attagirl!" April said. "I hope you threw him out on his ear."

Rita stirred uncomfortably. "Not right away. He stayed long enough to tell me my mother had nothing to do with his sticking around after he said hello for the first time. That all he'd originally intended to do last night was to say a proper good night."

"What was going on before the telephone call sounds as if whatever he was doing was a darn good good-night performance," April sighed. "For a lady who spouts the importance of sexual attraction, you sure are naive. What did you expect the guy would do after an invitation to visit your apartment? Just have a cup of coffee and leave?"

Rita felt herself color again. "I know, I know. Actually, we never got around to having coffee. And what happened between us was not entirely unexpected. In fact, I wanted it."

April and Rita exchanged knowing glances.

"So what's your problem?" April asked.

"What would be the point of falling in love with a man I'd have to spend the rest of my life worrying about? Furthermore, his life is in Texas, and mine is here in Chicago."

April sobered. "I'm afraid that's a problem no one can help you with. If you love Colby and he loves you, maybe you can get him to move and change his profession. Well, I've got to go back to work." She gestured to the roses. "No matter what you decide, you must have done something right last night, or Colby wouldn't be sending you flowers this morning." She paused at the door. "By the way, what did the card that came with the roses say?"

Rita blushed again. "All it said was good night."

Lili's mouth fell open in awe. "Wow," she said. "That's *so* romantic."

"Maybe," April said. "If there's anything I know about men, especially men like my Lucas and your Colby, is that while they might appear to be Sullivans on the outside, on the inside they're pussycats. Take it from me, all that's needed is the right woman to turn them into believers. If you remember, Lucas was a hard case until I gave him a few lessons to show him how wrong he was about those six rules of his. As for Colby, if you want my opinion, I think the guy is more than interested in you. So go get him. That is, if you still want him."

"I'm not sure," Rita answered as she straightened a drooping rose. "Sometimes I think I don't really know Colby."

"Come on now," April scoffed. "You've already said you've known Colby almost all your life. How could you not know each other?"

"Maybe because we're probably not the same people we were ten years ago."

"That's what you were trying to prove last night, wasn't it?" Rita nodded. "Then there's no problem," April said airily. "Colby has to have noticed the difference in you or he wouldn't be sending you roses. Take it from someone who's learned how to handle a man who came from another planet and brought him into this one—you haven't seen the last of him."

THREE LONG DAYS went by, with Rita trying to analyze Colby's attraction for her, when April's parting words came true.

"Hey!" Arthur said as he rolled his cart into Rita's office. "I've just come up from the mail room. Take a look at what came for you today!"

Rita glanced away from her computer with a frown. She'd been lost in surfing the magazine's archives for yesterday's politicians involved in crime and had just uncovered a snippet of information she was sure Colby would be interested in. "Of all the times to play games, now isn't one of them, Arthur. I'm really busy here."

"It's no joke," Arthur said gleefully. "The card that came with it has your name on it."

It turned out to be a wicker basket decorated with red ribbon, Christmas ornaments and mistletoe. Arthur lifted it off the cart and onto a corner of her desk.

A red-and-white-checkered cloth peeped out from the corners of the basket, but the aroma that wafted into the office gave the contents away.

"A picnic basket?" Rita undid the bright red ribbons, the miniature Christmas decorations, lifted the top of the basket and gazed in awe at its contents. There was a container of hard-boiled eggs, a jar of caviar, assorted cheeses, a baguette, small sausages, an assortment of pastries and a cluster of purple grapes. Real glasses, dishes and cutlery were tucked in corners.

"Goodness! This is amazing."

"Sure is," Arthur said as he eyed the basket enviously. "Whoever sent it went all out."

"Yeah, I did," Colby said as he sauntered into the office. "We're having a picnic breakfast." To Rita's surprise, he carried a small blanket and a couple of pillows. He was dressed in black jeans, a flannel shirt and a heavy corduroy jacket and boots and looked ready for the outdoors. "Since it's beginning to snow outside, I'm beginning to rethink the possibility of our going to a park."

Rita was speechless, but not for long. Roses the other day, a basket of breakfast goodies and an invitation to picnic on a December morning?

If all this was merely in the name of friendship, her name wasn't Rita Rosales.

She gestured to the vase of roses. "You sent the roses the other day, didn't you? Why? And before you answer, I'd like to know what else you have in mind."

Colby shrugged. "Whatever it takes."

Rita's eyes narrowed. "Whatever it takes to do what?"

"To make amends for the other night?" he said with a pointed look at Arthur. "The first thing is to decide where we're going to have breakfast."

Rita found herself seriously considering the question before she caught herself. If Arthur hadn't been gaping in the background, or if Colby hadn't looked so self-assured, she would have flown into Colby's arms and shown him that breakfast anywhere was okay with her. It didn't seem to matter anymore if he was a true Sullivan or not. He was here this morning and that's all that mattered.

At her silence, Colby said to Arthur, "Thanks for bringing up the basket. Is there anything else you want to deliver? If not…"

Arthur flushed, shook his head and backed out of the office.

"Now, where were we…?" With Arthur gone, Colby glanced around the small office. One wall of shelves and several small tables held a clutter of reference books, newspapers and magazines. A computer, a monitor and yellow legal pads covered with annotations filled the desk. A printer sat on a stand beside it. The photograph of Rita at her friend's wedding was gone.

"This doesn't look like a real library any more than you look like a librarian, Ri," he said with an admiring glance at her beige slacks, matching jacket and green sweater. "Are you sure you're legit?"

"I keep telling you my name is Rita and I'm legit

all right," Rita said, distracted by the look in Colby's eyes. "Besides, I'm not a library librarian. I'm a research librarian. And by the way, I've just come across something interesting in the magazine's archives you might be interested in."

"Later," Colby said as he looked for a place to put the blanket and pillow. "As for where to go for breakfast, we could have it right here."

Rita glanced around her cluttered office. "You're joking! A breakfast picnic here in my office?"

"Easy," Colby said. "All we have to do is close the shades, lock the door, pull the plug on the telephone and find a flat surface."

Wide-eyed, Rita stole a glance at the cluttered but flat surface of her desk, then to the only small, clear space—a corner on the floor. Visions of what Colby might have meant by a flat surface brought a rush of heat to her face. She hoped Colby didn't notice.

He did. "Tsk, tsk," he chided. "I wouldn't have thought you capable of such thoughts." He came around the desk, planted himself in front of her. "Trust me. It's not what you're thinking."

"What I'm thinking isn't the problem," Rita said breathlessly as she backed away from temptation. She didn't need to wonder how she really felt about Colby. She knew. She'd fallen for him, hook, line and sinker. From the twinkle in his eyes, the dratted man knew it. "The problem here is what *you're* thinking."

Unrepentant, Colby took a step toward her. "Maybe so, but that *is* what you wanted me to think the other night, wasn't it? That is, before your mother's telephone call changed your mind?"

Chagrined at having him read her thoughts as if they were written on her forehead, Rita took another step backward. "Oh, I don't know."

"You forget, I've known you forever," he said as he reached to push back a wisp of hair that had fallen over her cheek. "The look on your face always gave you away when you were a kid, and the look on your face is giving you away now." His eyes roamed over her. "Except maybe in some important ways that count." He took another step toward her.

"Now, see here, Colby," Rita protested, stopped with her back literally against the wall. "I don't care what your intentions are, we just can't have a picnic breakfast here. If you want breakfast, there's always the cafeteria. This *is* a business office. I have work to do!"

"Maybe so," Colby said with a calculated glance that sent Rita's senses spinning all over again. "There has to be somewhere suitable for a picnic. Of course," he went on, "I'm sure we *could* stay right here if you really wanted to. After all, I'm only talking about having breakfast together."

Just breakfast! Not if she read the look in Colby's eyes right. She had an uneasy feeling he was out to teach her a lesson. And heaven help her, she was a willing pupil.

She hesitated long enough to smother thoughts that made every nerve in her body tingle in anticipation.

"Forget playing games, Colby. Just lay it on the line and come out with what this is all about. Why would you want to have breakfast? You could have waited until lunchtime to have lunch. That's only a couple of hours from now."

When Colby eyed her thoughtfully, she knew he was aware of the turmoil going through her. "The fact is, I have a lot of work ahead of me," she went on. "I'm not kidding."

Colby sat down on the corner of her desk. "Neither am I. I won't give up until I get a chance to properly apologize for what happened the other night in your apartment."

"Nothing happened the other night," Rita retorted and swallowed the lump in her throat. "You have nothing to apologize for. It was my fault for inviting you up to my apartment. Even if my mother hadn't called, I should have realized we were too grown-up to play games."

"Games? Personally, I thought that whatever was going on was pretty grown-up. Of course," he added with a grin, "maybe that's the trouble here. Maybe we need to back off and find a middle ground. As I said the other night, I *would* like to think we're friends before I have to leave."

Rita's heart began to waltz to three-quarter time. How could she be just a friend to a man she was already in love with?

To really muddle Colby's proposed friendship scenario, she had to be honest, if not with him at least with herself. The truth was, she hadn't been able to think clearly from the moment Colby had shown up at her office door. Mere friendship between them was out.

But as long as she wasn't sure how he felt about her, she was too proud to show how she felt about him. "Under the circumstances, I suppose breakfast is a good idea. You're sure?"

"Yep. The only problem is," he added, "if you're right about my being followed, and I'm beginning to think you are, we'll have to go somewhere where we can hide in plain sight."

"Not until I know *why* you have to hide in plain sight."

"Well, I can tell you this—the locals who've been bringing immigrants up from Mexico aren't too happy with me." He shrugged. "But hey, I'm not too happy with them, either."

Rita considered. She was positive Colby had been stalked, only she hadn't known why. "Okay," she finally agreed. She couldn't let Colby disappear for another ten years. Not without cheating herself of something she'd yearned for most of her life. "I'm sure I can think of someplace."

"Wait a minute," Colby said, gazing around the office. "Let's go back to my first idea. Here in your office is the safest place I can think of."

Rita stared at him. A breakfast picnic in her office was sounding more inviting by the minute. With the blinds closed, no one would know what was going on inside....

Chapter Ten

"I take it your silence is a yes?"

"No—" Rita scowled "—it's a maybe."

"So," Colby said, "how long do you think it will take for you to decide?"

Rita thought fast. If breakfast was really all he had in mind, she had nothing to lose but an hour of her time. If he had any more personal plans than breakfast, he was in for a surprise. She was a lot wiser this morning than she'd been the other night.

This wasn't her apartment where, if she looked through the windows, there were stars shining on the dark mirror that was Lake Michigan. Or an intimate setting where moonlight streaming in through the window had turned her apartment into a world where two people could rediscover each other in intimate ways. This was a business office where people passed by her door.

At last she nodded. "Yeah, why not," she said as if a breakfast on her office floor was an everyday occurrence. Underneath her casual smile her thoughts were in turmoil. Friendship was something personal, sometimes very close, but from the way Colby was looking at her she was pretty sure friendship wasn't all he had in mind. Now was the time to find out just what he *did* have in mind.

"Go ahead and set things up. I'll be with you in a minute." She unplugged her telephone, closed the blinds, then caught her breath when Colby reached to retrieve a Do Not Disturb sign she'd brought home from a brief vacation a year ago and hung it on the outside of the door. She started to protest, then reconsidered. Instead, she picked up a notice of the office Christmas party next Saturday night and pretended to study it so that she wouldn't look too interested.

By the time she turned back to Colby, he'd cleared a corner of the office floor and was carefully spreading the blanket. With a speculative glance at her, he fluffed the pillows, set them on the floor beside him and held out his hand.

"Breakfast, my lady."

Grateful she'd dressed in pants today, not a skirt, Rita took Colby's hand and dropped onto one of the pillows. "What now?"

"Hold on a minute." He lifted a glass container of orange juice out of the basket, shook it and poured her a glass. "I'm sure you're going to like this. At least it's not as potent as a margarita."

Rita sipped the fresh juice and covertly glanced at

her watch. A breakfast picnic on her office floor was an incongruous event in itself; picnicking with Colby was another.

Just looking at his confident smile sent shivers up and down her spine. She took another sip of orange juice to hide what she was feeling.

"Tastes good, doesn't it?" he asked.

Rita settled for a noncommittal shrug and another sip. The more slowly she traveled down the road that led to intimacy with him, the more easily she'd be able to retreat.

Provided she still wanted to retreat.

She honestly didn't know.

She pulled a cloth napkin from the basket to use as a place mat and studied the rest of the basket's contents. When Colby gallantly gestured for her to help herself, her stomach rebelled.

Caviar at ten in the morning?

After her usual hurried breakfast of toast and coffee this morning, even the bland and conveniently peeled hard-boiled eggs didn't look tempting. Resisting a shudder, she broke off a small piece of the baguette and made a show of eating.

"Smells good," Colby said with a frown at the small spicy turkey sausages, "but I'd hardly call this food for a man." He contemplated the jar of caviar and shook his head. "The salesman at the deli recommended this stuff, but now that I look at it, I think I should have chosen the menu myself."

With her food preferences usually running more to the Tex-Mex she'd been raised on, Rita was inclined to agree. Still, the menu wasn't what was bothering her. It was Colby.

Years in the outdoors had given his skin a golden sheen that accented his clear brown eyes. His hair was a little long at the neckline, but on him it looked manly. The boyhood cowlick she remembered still seemed determined to fall over his forehead. He was familiar, yet a stranger.

A stranger she wanted to know.

More to the point, before matters went too far, she still wanted to know more about the business that had brought him to Chicago. His vague comment about the locals bringing immigrants up from Mexico not being happy with him wasn't enough. He was being threatened, and so was she, if only by association, and she wanted to know more. She had a *right* to know more, didn't she?

"So, Ri...I mean Rita," he said with a smile of apology, "do you think we can still be friends?"

To protect her too-vulnerable heart, she decided to play along. "Of course we can be friends," she said airily. "Just so long as you lay off those Texas welcomes and goodbyes every time you plan to pass through Chicago."

His eyebrows arched. "Friends say hello and sometimes they have to say goodbye whether they want to or not. What's wrong with that?"

Colby tried to look innocent, but since Rita remembered the young Colby, she knew better. "Nothing, if friendship is all you have in mind. I happen to think you have other plans."

Colby's expression didn't change as he took another swallow of his juice. "I keep telling you, I'm only trying to be friendly."

"Yeah, right! Your kiss the other night implied a lot more than that! So did your words!"

For Colby, the last ten years disappeared in a wink. Rita's predictable reaction to his teasing reminded him of the old days when they were kids back in Sunrise. He probably liked the new Rita more than was good for him....

"Oh, Rita," he said as he tried to ignore his stirring body, "I wouldn't do anything you didn't want me to do. I really want us to be friends. I swear."

Rita worried her lower lip. Her problem seemed to be that friendship wasn't what she wanted. She wanted *him.*

Colby smiled and reached into the basket and came up with a grape he held to her lips. "Try this. Maybe it will make you feel better."

Instinctively Rita opened her mouth, and Colby leaned forward and popped in the fruit. "Although," he said, "I have a better idea."

He took the glass of orange juice out of her nerveless fingers and, to her surprise, the better idea turned out to be a kiss. If this was friendship, Rita thought dimly as her body responded to his touch, it was okay with her. Especially since Colby's unfinished goodbye the other night had left her wanting. Desperately wanting.

So she did what she'd started to do the other night. She put her arms around his neck and raised her lips for another kiss.

He didn't disappoint her. His arms were firm and sure as he gathered her to him and sat back against the wall with her in his lap. To add to the magic of the moment, his lips tasted sweetly of oranges.

"Like I said the other night, this is a heck of a lot better than arguing," he finally murmured into the nape of her neck.

Rita felt her herself sink into a warm sea of pleasurable sensations—until voices outside the door reminded her that this was her office, not her apartment. Anyone, including the magazine's owner, Tom Eldridge, could have easily taken the sign on the door as a joke and walked into the office.

More to the point, she thought as she rested her forehead against Colby's shoulder long enough to catch her breath, even though the road to intimacy was more pleasurable than she'd ever suspected, it was still a road she was determined not to travel.

Not yet.

Hadn't Colby made it clear he only wanted to be her friend, that he was just passing through Chicago? She had to keep reminding herself that the man she hoped to travel down the road to intimacy with wasn't Colby.

She'd been a child back in Sunrise, surrounded by a protective family. Some years ago, she'd decided it was time to come to Chicago in search of herself and had become an independent woman. She intended to act like one.

She pulled out of Colby's arms and struggled to her feet. "You sure do give the word *friendship* a new dimension," she managed to say as she tried to calm her racing heart. "I think it's time for us to have a serious talk."

Colby frowned and sat back, taking a dim view of any immediate need of Rita's to talk. He would have given a lot to be able to pull her back into his arms and show her just what his idea of a real friendship could mean—if only she were willing. Until he remembered that Rita had a will of steel and a temper to match. From the way she stood there looking down at him, that much about her hadn't changed.

Besides, he thought ruefully, Rita was right. For old times' sake, and because he actually cared what she thought about him, he owed her the whole truth. And she would know the whole truth of why he was here in Chicago—when he was free to tell her. Soon.

"I take it the picnic's over?"

"Right," Rita said. She marched to the door, opened it a crack, reached for the Do Not Disturb sign, took it off and closed the door again. The blinds were next.

She turned back to Colby and gestured to the blanket. "I've just realized I'm not really in the mood for a picnic after all. What I do want is to know *all* about what's going on here and I want to know now!"

"Well, I'm hungry even if you're not," Colby replied, ignoring her demand. "Working at trying to be friends makes a guy ravenous," he said with a forced grin. She didn't budge.

Regretfully, Colby glanced at the food left in the basket. Obviously she wasn't impressed.

"I'm willing to go somewhere to have this talk you want," he said with a shrug, "but only if I get to have lunch later. To show you I mean it, you can choose the place."

"Well, I'm back to thinking about a place where you can 'hide in plain sight.' I know the perfect place."

Colby rose and reached for her hand. "Okay. Let's go."

"I know you think I'm being foolish," Rita said as she helped pack up the picnic basket, "but I care what happens to you. Considering you're a lawman who should know more about criminals than I do, so should you."

Colby had to agree. Rita was right, but he wasn't prepared to tell her so. It would only make her worry about him even more. "So where to?"

"Navy Pier."

Colby shook his head. "Provided you turn out to be right about my being followed, I'm not ready to get the feds involved in this."

"I wasn't talking about the federal government," she laughed. Having just finished researching local crime activity, Rita knew that anyone aiding illegal immigrants was guilty of a federal crime. She stashed Colby's remark about involving the federal government in the back of her mind to explore at a later time. "Navy Pier is actually a theme park first opened in 1916 and was used during the Second World War as a military training site," she explained. "That's how it got its name. The area is popular with tourists and is located right on Lake Michigan. If you don't think there are enough people to hide behind, there's also Gateway Park just west of the pier."

"Nope, the pier sounds good enough. The more people and the more activity the better," Colby said as he hefted the picnic basket. "That's the whole idea of HIPS—hiding in plain sight."

Rita still felt a smidgen of doubt. "It seems to me the more crowded a place, the harder it's going to be for you to notice any suspicious activity."

"Like I said, HIPS is a proven strategy, especially in witness protection programs," Colby said patiently. "I figure I'm a witness—sort of."

He studied the expression on Rita's face. "If you're going to look for dangerous activity under every rock, maybe it would be smarter for us to stay right here."

"No way!" Rita reached into a drawer and took out her purse. "Since this strategy calls for someone who knows how the minds of criminals work, you're on. I'm willing to try."

"I do, and thank you for trusting me. So tell me, is this Navy Pier another Disneyland?"

Rita laughed at the interest in Colby's voice. "Not unless you count the Ferris wheel and the carousel. The whole development is a lot more than just an amusement park. You'll see when we get there."

"Oops, I forgot. It's starting to snow out there. Might keep the tourists away."

"No problem," Rita replied. "Some years, the snow is so deep we can hardly move in it. Other years, like this one, there's hardly enough snow to make a snowball."

"Great. We can always talk on the Ferris wheel. No one would think of looking for us there."

At the thought of being one hundred and fifty feet high above Chicago's skyline surrounded by empty space, Rita grabbed her stomach. "No way! You'll have to think of someplace else or I'm staying right here."

Colby put his arm around her shoulders and hugged her. "Sorry about that. I'm afraid I clean forgot you're afraid of heights. But don't worry. I promise to take good care of you, Ri."

Hardly mollified, Rita managed to ignore the use of her nickname and searched in her purse for her car keys. Colby might intend to take care of her, but who, if not herself, was going to take care of him?

HE'D BEEN RIGHT about the snow keeping tourists away, but there were still enough people around for his plan to work, Colby thought as he sniffed appreciatively at the tantalizing scent wafting from the numerous fast-food restaurants that lined the main street of Navy Pier. Because the temperature hovered around freezing, most of the snow had melted when it hit the ground. What was left had been cleared away into small snowbanks.

He noticed that even though most of the park's attractions were closed for the winter for maintenance, Christmas decorations hung on lampposts. Overhead, loudspeakers blared Christmas carols.

A few pedestrians strolling down the street and, thank goodness, an occasional restaurant or bar was still open. Still, he had second thoughts. Maybe Navy Pier wasn't the place to hide in plain sight, after all.

He inhaled the scent of hot dogs, the cool, clean air and turned back to Rita. "Since I didn't get a chance to finish breakfast, I'm in favor of finding someplace to eat before we chat."

"Good grief, Colby," Rita said impatiently as she buttoned the top of her jacket and hurried ahead of him. "If you were that hungry, you should have brought the picnic basket with us."

Colby grimaced at her mention of the picnic basket. "A working man needs something more filling than hard boiled eggs, caviar and cheese."

Rita snorted. "A *working* man? Ha!"

Colby gazed pointedly at a small nearby fast-food restaurant. "I think better on a full stomach. Preferably with a Philly cheese steak sandwich, fries and a cold beer, but if you're not interested..." he said as he looked longingly at a hot-dog stand.

"I'm not! Like I said, there's something more important going on here, and I intend to find out what it is before the day is through."

Colby groaned. "I suppose I can wait if I have to."

Undeterred by the forlorn look on his face, Rita took Colby's arm and drew him into a knot of people waiting to get into the IMAX theater where it was warm. "How's this?"

"Not good. You're not supposed to talk in a theater," Colby said when the couple next to them began to grumble at their intrusion. "What's next?"

"I'm thinking," Rita said as she smiled her apology to the pair and started down the street. "There has to be a likely place to have that talk you promised me. And," she added firmly as she pushed her way through the small group of people going into the fast-food restaurant, "after all this effort to hide in plain sight, it had better be someplace good."

"Rita," Colby said with a longing look at the golden arches of a McDonald's, "just who do you think would be following me down here?"

"Maybe the same two men who followed you before," Rita muttered. "I don't have to be a Texas Ranger to know those two can put one and one together and realize we know each other. Especially after both of us appeared on Horton's television show together."

"Your point is?" Colby asked uneasily. How on earth had he come up with the idea that appearing on a television program would be hiding in plain sight?

He'd suspected Rita was getting too close to the truth for his comfort, but he hadn't realized just how close. If he was being tailed, it was his fault for falling for Rita and forgetting a Ranger creed never to become involved with someone while on assignment.

"It's simple. All anyone would have to do is to follow me in order to find you."

Colby felt a chill pass over him. Considering his training and experience, how in the hell had he not realized from the get-go that just by looking up Rita, he could be placing her in jeopardy? Or that their joint appearance on Horton's, designed to show he was merely a tourist friend passing through Chicago on his way home could backfire?

He glanced at Rita. The winds coming off Lake Michigan were blowing her silken, ebony hair around her face while was she was covertly checking people passing by. Reminded of their reason for being here, Colby forced his mind off his testosterone and joined her in surveying their surroundings.

As far as he could tell, while there were all shapes, size and colors of pedestrians, no one looked especially menacing.

Maybe Rita *would* feel better if she knew more about why he was in Chicago, he thought. Instead of wondering about his next meal, it was time to tell Rita the whole story so she would be prepared in case anything happened. What could happen, he didn't know, but he sure hoped to hell nothing would.

He spied a miniature-golf course where a few players willing to brave the cold were slicing balls through fallen snow. Maybe this was a good place to talk. "Come on, Ri. How about a game of miniature golf?"

"Golf?" Rita sputtered to a stop. "How are we going to have a serious conversation while we're chasing a golf ball around?"

"Because there are people moving around out there. The whole idea is to keep moving. It's not easy to hit a moving target."

"Great," Rita muttered. "That's what I've always wanted to grow up to become—a moving target!" She pulled out of Colby's grasp and gazed around her.

Her only choices were the Smith Museum of Stained Glass Windows, the Chicago Shakespeare Theater and an English pub, none of which, as far as she was concerned, fit the bill for hiding in plain sight. "I have a better idea. How about a ride on the carousel?"

"*That's* your idea of hiding?" Colby said, unable to believe his ears. "Heck, that's not much better than playing miniature golf! At least my feet would be on firm ground."

She grabbed his arm. "Come on, the carousel is the perfect place for HIPS. We'll be moving all the time."

"Aw, come on, Ri." Colby gazed longingly at the little golf course. "A carousel's for kids."

"Not true," Rita said. "The ride is a favorite of mine. All we have to do is see if it's still open. No one will think of looking for us there."

Rita took him by his elbow and led him protesting in the direction of the carousel. "Maybe I can catch the brass ring," she added.

Colby almost groaned at the look of pleasure on Rita's face. He couldn't bring himself to tell her he wasn't any happier at going around in circles than she was about heights. Especially on an empty stomach. Still, if riding to nowhere was all it took to put that smile on her winsome face, he was game. "Are you sure you don't get motion sickness?"

"You do?"

"Yeah, but if it makes you happy, I'll do it," he added when Rita looked concerned.

She hesitated. "Just to show you my heart's in the right place, I'll buy you a hot dog as soon as the ride is over. That ought to keep you until lunch. But not," she added firmly, "before you've told me the whole story behind what you're doing here."

"Is that a promise?" Colby tried to resist the impulse to kiss her. He thought back to the unfinished breakfast picnic back in Rita's office. Gazing at her now, all he could think of was how her lips had tasted.

He covered a sigh with a rueful grin. "If it *is* a promise, Ri, I intend to hold you to it. I know you want me to call you Rita, but the truth is," he said with a playful wink, "you'll always be Ri to me."

"It's a promise." Touched that Colby seemed to sense there *was* a bond beyond friendship growing between them, Rita smiled back. If Colby only knew. He might be talking about her promising him a hot dog, but she was promising him her heart.

Chapter Eleven

The carousel sat empty and silent when Rita and Colby arrived. A worker was brushing snowflakes off the horses and inspecting leather harnesses. A lone mechanic was tinkering with the carousel's motor.

"Oh, dear!" Rita looked longingly at the carousel. "I guess this ride, too, is down for maintenance at this time of the year."

Colby was about to suggest moving on, when he saw the wistful longing on Rita's face. She might be a grown woman, but when it came to riding carousels, the child in her obviously prevailed. He had to do something to put a smile on her face.

"Hang on a minute, I'll be right back." Colby left Rita standing by a pretty brown-and-white horse, jumped on the carousel and made his way between the rows of horses to where the mechanic was working. "Any chance of starting up any time soon?"

"Nah." The man put down his wrench and wiped his hands on an oily towel. "We're doing the annual winter maintenance checkup. I'm about to go to lunch. Why?"

Colby gestured to Rita. "We're from out of town," he said with his fingers mentally crossed. "My girlfriend had her heart set on a ride. I hate to see her disappointed. What'll it take to start up for a few minutes to make her happy?"

The mechanic glanced around as if to make sure they weren't being watched, thought for a few minutes, then shrugged. "What'll you offer?"

"A free lunch, maybe a beer or two?"

"Done!" The man stashed the grimy towel in a bucket and reached for the carousel's controls. "Just make it quick. Don't want the boss to know!"

Colby took his wallet out of his pocket, peeled off a twenty and handed it to the man. "Thanks. Give me a minute to get my girlfriend on her horse."

He made his way back to where Rita was waiting. "Climb on. I've just rented the carousel."

She didn't waste time arguing. She reached for the pole that anchored the horse. "For how long?"

"Long enough."

He tried to ignore her shapely backside as she swung onto her chosen steed.

The canned organ music began to play the "Carousel Waltz" and the carousel started to revolve. Rita looked at him. "You're getting on one, too, aren't you?"

Colby glanced over to where the mechanic was giving him a thumbs-up. He mounted the black-and-white horse next to Rita that, happily rose when hers went down. As for any meaningful conversation between himself and Rita, not a chance. Not when they never moved in sync.

Beside him, Rita hummed along with the music. Twenty dollars had been cheap to put the smile back on her face. He would have doubled it if he'd had to in order to put it there.

Happily, Rita caught the brass ring the second time around. Even more happily for Colby, who felt like an overgrown kid, the carousel slowed to a stop.

He waved his thanks to the mechanic and climbed off his horse just as Rita swung off hers. "Happy?" he asked.

She held up the brass ring. "Yes, but what do I do with this?"

When a snowflake drifted on to the tip of Rita's nose, Colby resisted the urge to kiss it away, to have it melt on his tongue and to use it as an excuse to get close enough to take her in his arms. Something he intended to do as soon as he got her home, he reminded himself when he remembered they were out in the open. Instead, he pulled her arm through his. "Why don't you keep it as a good-luck charm."

"Good luck? That reminds me—how can I watch your back if I don't know what's going on?"

Watch his back! As long as Rita seemed determined to help him, Colby despaired of being able to keep them out of trouble. At the rate she was burrowing into his affairs, he had to do something drastic to call her off before one or both of them got hurt.

He blamed himself, and not for the first time. If he'd only paid her the visit her mother wanted and gone his own way, instead of claiming a Texas welcome for his efforts, Rita wouldn't have been involved in this mess.

Or if he hadn't persuaded himself he needed to appear on Paul Horton's show for Rita's sake, he'd be long gone underground by now.

What it did amount to was that, even though he knew hanging around Rita wasn't the brightest idea he'd ever come up with, he couldn't get enough of her.

But what he hated to tell Rita was that it looked as if he'd come too close to his target for her safety and comfort. Or that they were being watched meant matters were bound to come to a head soon. The covert operation in Chicago wasn't his first underground assignment, and it wasn't going to be his last. Not by a long shot.

He quietly checked out the surrounding territory. With the snow flurries gradually turning into real snow, it looked as if most of the tourists brave enough to visit the park in this weather had left for warmer pleasures. So far, so good.

He would have been a wiser and certainly happier man if he could have been sure nothing dangerous would happen while he and Rita were together.

He turned his gaze back to her. A frown had replaced her smile. If she was thinking about him, it didn't look as if her thoughts were all hearts and flowers.

When it came to Rita, his were.

She was a woman out of his past who had begun to mean more to him than he'd anticipated. Considering his profession, he had no business even toying with the idea that she could become part of his future.

More for her sake than for his.

He didn't look forward to having to go underground tonight, but he didn't have much choice. He'd been debriefed by Lieutenant Bruner, his counterpart in the Chicago Police Department, and the results had been clear. He had to say goodbye to Rita sooner or later, preferably sooner.

As much as he would have loved to explore an intimate relationship with her, honor and sworn duty came first.

He'd been in tighter situations than this before, he reminded himself as they walked along under gently drifting snowflakes. But never before with someone who meant as much to him as Rita. He'd only skimmed the surface when he'd told her why he was in Chicago. The whole story went on to include immigrant workers who were being killed before they could testify against organized-crime syndicates, or the "coyotes" who'd brought them to Chicago. Without their parents, small children were being abandoned to make it on their own. Theft and robbery were at an all-time high.

If Rita so much as heard about the lost children, nothing would stop her from trying to help.

The immediate problem was to tell her just enough so that she could at least be forewarned. But not enough to frighten her. The two incidents at La Paloma and Melvin's Diner had been bad enough. With or without Rita, he wasn't looking forward to more trouble.

Her hand in Colby's, Rita gazed fondly at him, admiring the firm set of his jaw, and his unruly shock of hair—not to mention the way he kept trying to brush it out of his eyes only to have it fall back again. He was definitely a man any woman would be proud to call her own.

But even as her heart told her that she might have found the man she'd been waiting for, she realized Colby might not feel the same way about her. Sure, he seemed to enjoy coming up with Texas embraces, but he enjoyed teasing her, too.

"Satisfied?"

Rita blinked. When they were children, Colby had always seemed to guess what she was thinking. Could he possibly know what she was thinking now?

She felt herself color. "About what?"

"The carousel ride," he said with a glance at her that made a wave of heat run through her.

"Of course."

"Okay," he said. "Now it's your turn to keep your promise."

Rita was so taken by the amused look in Colby's eyes, she couldn't remember which promise he was talking about. Whatever he had in mind, she was embarrassed to realize she could hardly wait to find out. "Which promise was that?"

"The hot dog," he said as he brushed an ebony tendril away from her cheek with a playful forefinger. "Don't tell me you've forgotten?"

"Oh, that." Suddenly Rita stopped. "Hey, wait a second. The deal was, you were going to tell me the whole story about why you're in Chicago first."

"Oh, yeah, that," he said grimly. "But after that carousel ride, I'm hungrier than ever. I can't talk on an empty stomach."

The woeful look in his eyes made her cave in. "Okay, first the hot dog, then…"

"Actually," he said as the reality of their being seen together out in the open again sank in, "I think we might be pressing our luck if we hang around here. I think we should try for somewhere more private." He pulled her closer and drew her hand through his arm.

Rita nodded. Her senses had never before been stirred the way Colby's touch was stirring her now.

"If you're really serious about being hungry, how about chicken?" She gestured to a sign advertising fifty-four kinds of chicken dinners from broiled to Southern fried and fifty-two different varieties in between. "That ought to be a good place for us to hide."

"That's better than caviar and sausages," he answered with a regretful eye on a sidewalk hot-dog vendor. "But as long as you're giving me a choice, frankly, a steak sounds better than chicken."

Rita stopped long enough to check out the other restaurants lining the walkway. "I'm sure there's a steak house somewhere along here. Maybe we can—"

The hair on the back of Colby's neck tingled when Rita's voice broke off. His sixth sense kicked in as his gaze swept their surroundings. Sure enough, two men, one wearing a cowboy hat with a small red feather in the brim, had appeared across the horizon. Although the red feather wasn't an unusual adornment on a cowboy hat, he already knew it was an organized-crime sign, identifying the same group who escorted illegal immigrants up from the border and dropped them off at various points on the way to Chicago.

"Hurry, Ri. We've got to move!" He took her arm and quickened his steps until they reached a brick wall. It felt as if the muscles in Rita's arm had turned to ice. The fright in her eyes was unmistakable.

Rita's sightings had been real all along, although for her sake, he'd been wary of admitting it. Just as the look of terror on her face was real now.

Thank God they were standing in front of a wall where no one could sneak up behind them. Instinctively, he stepped in front of Rita and pushed her behind his back.

"Ri? Take a quick look to your right, but don't expose yourself. Are those the same two men you saw before?"

"Yes!" she whispered. He could feel her shivering into his shoulder. "It looks as if they're headed this way."

Without moving from in front of Rita, Colby's gaze swiveled to three o'clock. He was just in time to see the two men turn and run in the opposite direction.

He started to go after them, then stopped. If he gave chase, he'd have to leave Rita alone and unprotected.

Maybe that was what the men wanted him to do!

He couldn't, it was only a matter of time before they'd come back for Rita.

Refusing to be taken in by the possible ruse to draw him away from Rita, Colby vowed he'd stay close to her until he got her safely back to her apartment. She had work at her office maybe, but he wanted her in the safest place possible.

"Let's go," he said after a last, hurried glance around the park. "I'm taking you home. And I want you to stay there."

Furthermore, he vowed before he went back underground, he intended to make sure the Chicago Police Department provided a bodyguard for Rita. At least until he was able to could come back and take care of her himself.

Rita dug in her heels. "Now that your HIPS theory hasn't worked, I'm not going to leave without finding someplace private where we can have that talk. You owe me a more detailed explanation about why you're in Chicago than you've given me!"

An explanation wasn't all he owed her or all she owed him, Colby thought as he threw a protective arm around her shoulders. There was still that other unfinished business between them…and it had nothing to do with illegal immigration.

A glance at the determined expression on Rita's face told him that at the moment Texas-style embraces were the furthest thing from her mind.

"I will tell you some," Colby said as he tried to hurry her along the main walkway. If she only knew how much trouble they were in, maybe she wouldn't be so eager to help. "But not because I intend to let you help me."

Damn, he thought. He'd sure had his priorities backward. Here he was in Chicago, in an almost deserted park, dodging the unknown, when he'd been aware from the start that there'd be danger.

If his superiors knew what he'd gotten the pair of them into, he'd be drummed out of the Rangers for sure.

"And before you say anything," Rita said, warding off an appeal to her common sense one more time, "I'm definitely not about to go home!"

Colby suppressed the desire to pick her up, throw her over his shoulder and carry her home—maybe all the way to Sunrise, if necessary. He'd never have succeeded.

Still, first things first. Now that Rita was determined to help him, he had to tell her just enough of the facts to keep her out of trouble. Then, he'd take her back to her apartment and leave her there with someone to watch over her no matter how much she protested.

"So where to?" he said. "And make it quick. I'm starving."

"Follow me." Rita pointed to the Shakespeare theater. "There's a small English pub next to the theater. I doubt anyone would think of looking for us in there."

"Good enough for now," Colby muttered. "I hope you're right."

While he knew that the shortest distance between two points was a straight line drawn between them, he didn't intend to do something that might put them in danger. He decided the quick route he'd requested wasn't a good idea. "You follow *me*. We're going to the pub, but we're going to do it my way."

Colby's way was to stroll nonchalantly through the few curious people who were braving the snow. With Rita's hand held tightly in his just in case she had any other ideas and ran, he headed for a small rose garden with an unpainted and weather-worn garden shed off to one side.

Before she had a chance to protest, he opened the door, shoved Rita inside, followed her in and bolted the door behind him.

"Good gravy! What are we doing in here, anyway?" Rita peered around the dimly lit structure.

Piles of compost and something else she didn't care to name filled a corner. Well-used gardening tools leaned against the wall in one corner, a wheelbarrow in another. Two baited mousetraps waited ominously on a potting bench. Even the spiderwebs hanging across the ceiling looked ominous. She moved closer to Colby.

"We're staying out of sight until I'm sure the coast is clear," Colby said as he peered through an open knothole. "I don't intend to have them figure out where we're headed."

Rita froze at the sound of male voices outside the shed. The thought that a gardener could force open the door at any moment and discover them inside sent more shivers up and down her spine.

"So far, so good," she finally heard Colby murmur. "I don't see anyone following us."

"Thank goodness!" Grateful, Rita moved even closer to Colby. "There has to be a nicer-smelling place to hide than this shed."

Colby peered through the knothole again. "Okay, we can get out of here."

"We're going straight to the pub, I hope," she muttered. "I could use some liquid courage."

Colby started to remind her what happened the last time she drank, then thought better of it. Besides, he needed a strong drink himself.

"First we're going to wander in and out a few of the fast-food places, the ones that are still open."

"Can't you make up your mind what you want to eat without doing that?"

Colby had to smile at Rita's frustration. "Only in order to throw off anyone who might be following us. When I'm sure no one's on our tail, we'll head for the pub."

"Get outta here!" Rita retorted. "I'm freezing!" After an uneasy silence, she finally put her hand in his. "Okay," she said. "But do you have any idea how many fast-food places there are around here?"

"Too many, but from what I've noticed, most of them are closed." Rita's hand felt like an ice cube. He took both her cold hands in his and gently rubbed them between his palms until he felt warmth return.

"That feels so good," Rita whispered as she cuddled into his warmth. "Please, Colby…."

Colby considered lingering long enough to find out just what Rita meant by "please," but the foul smell made him lead her out of the shed.

Twenty minutes later, after wandering in and out of the few restaurants with a reluctant Rita in tow, he said, "Okay, let's make a beeline for the pub."

"At last," she said fervently, then led the way.

"Just take it easy with the drinks," Colby teased. "We don't want you under the table again."

"Well, just don't forget we have unfinished business," Rita reminded him. "You have to tell me what's going on."

"How could I forget," Colby muttered.

Chapter Twelve

"I honestly think you ought to go back to Sunrise now," Colby urged when they found a secluded booth where he could keep a cautious eye on the door of the pub. "If I haven't convinced you to go home for Christmas, what just happened out there a few minutes ago—being followed by shady characters—ought to have changed your mind. Of course," he added with a grimace, "I know how stubborn you are."

"You're really out to lunch if you think I can be frightened into going back to Sunrise for Christmas or for any other reason," Rita said with a scowl. "My folks would only try to make me stay for good."

"You know, Ri, I need to tell you," Colby said, reaching over and touching her hand. "The real reason I asked you out to dinner was that, once I saw you in your office, I couldn't see myself settling for a hello and goodbye."

Rita blushed. "And that's why you tried to promote a Texas welcome?"

"It just seemed the natural thing to do," Colby said with a wink as he remembered the hug and the kiss. Just remembering how great Rita had felt in his arms filled him with a surge of desire and a twinge of regret. "To be honest, what really makes me feel like an ass," he went on, "is that it looks as if your being seen with me at La Paloma has put you in harm's way."

Rita's heartbeat went from a waltz to a tango. Maybe Colby actually did care for her after all. "But I'm just an innocent bystander."

Colby snorted. "Innocent? That'll be the day." He paused. "You've been dying to find out what I'm involved in from the day I walked into your office. I promised to tell you more when we got here to the pub, so here it is."

Colby took a deep breath. "I've already told you I'm involved in finding the people who're bringing illegal immigrants up from Mexico. And while I'm here, I'm on loan to the Chicago Police Department and the INS. The work's dangerous. We're dealing with a ruthless criminal element." He glanced around their surroundings. "I hope I don't have to ask you to keep that to yourself."

"Of course not!" Rita answered indignantly. "But I'm curious—why Chicago?"

Colby paused to gauge just how much more information he could tell her without the information turning into a carrot on a stick. "Because the Midwest with its massive need for unskilled labor seems to be a favorite destination."

"And you're here to do what, exactly?" Rita asked.

"Hang on a minute," Colby said. "True confessions can be a thirsty job. You start in on the peanuts while I go to the bar to get a couple of beers. The waiter seems to be ignoring us."

Rita dipped into the dish of peanuts as Colby spoke to the bartender. She wasn't surprised to hear him suggest he had a dangerous role in cracking the source of the illegal operation. He'd been a daredevil as a teenager, and it looked as if that much about him hadn't changed.

She studied the swinging doors leading to the adjoining Shakespeare Theater, the beautiful stained-glass windows that related the story of the knights of the round table and the colorfully decorated and lit Christmas tree in the corner. From where she was sitting, anyone who entered the pub was in clear view. No problem there.

Colby came back with two frosted glasses of beer and handed her one. After he'd taken a deep swallow of his, he sat back to survey his companion. God, she was beautiful. No wonder he couldn't think straight.

"Now that I've told you that, what else would you like to know?"

Rita pushed the bowl of peanuts away and got down to business. "How long have you been working with Immigration?"

"On and off for a couple of years," Colby answered. "Now, more than ever. Unfortunately, along with the increased illegal traffic, there's been a rise in crime, and it's been happening to the immigrants desperate to come to the States to earn money to send back home. They not only pay through the nose to get here, but if the guys bringing them here run into any trouble, too many of these poor immigrants wind up dead."

Rita shuddered. Those poor people, thinking they were coming to the land of milk and honey, and finding, instead, corruption and death. She could understand how Colby's work could be dangerous.

She turned her thoughts to surveying the menu printed on a board above the pub's bar where glasses hung upside down from railings. Dollar bills, of all things, were taped to the rafters with a sign saying the bills would be donated to a charity that fed the hungry. The large mirror at the back of the bar reflected bottles of imported beer and barrels of ale on shelves and under the counter. The scent of fresh-cut sharp cheese and tart apples mingled with the scent of ale and served to remind her she was hungry. "How about a ploughman's lunch while we talk?"

"Thought you'd never ask." He caught the waiter's attention and he gave the man their order.

Rita eyed him thoughtfully. "When you first showed up in my office I was doing some research on old Chicago politics. Remember?"

"Yeah, I remember." Colby took another swallow of beer. "What does that have to do with me?"

Rita took a sip of her own beer, then set it aside. "If you'll come with me back to my office, I'll show you what I'm talking about."

Colby shook his head. "No way. For all we know, someone could have staked out the building and seen us leave. They could be waiting for us to come back. I don't want to involve you any more than I already have, and I damn well don't want you to get hurt by trying to help me. Why don't you just go ahead and tell me what you want to show me?"

"I can't," Rita protested. "My memory of the details isn't that good. Besides, you need to see it printed out in black and white."

As the waiter brought their lunch, Colby asked Rita, "Are you saying you think you have relevant information?"

"Yep." She gathered her handbag and slid out of the booth. "Let's go right now. This can't wait."

"Hang on a second, Ri. If we go to your office now, there'll still be a lot of staff there. We need to look at this information undisturbed. So let's take our time eating lunch, and plan our arrival after five o'clock, okay?"

Rita sat down again. "You're right. And I'm starving."

THREE HOURS LATER, Colby took the driver's seat of her car and drove to the magazine's building in record time, parked in her designated parking space in the underground garage and led the way to the elevators.

Once inside her office, Rita closed the door. She pulled out the yellow legal pad on which she'd been taking research notes and turned on her computer to where she'd found the information she knew would interest Colby. "There—*that's* what I was talking about."

Colby peered at the screen. "All I see is a page of a newspaper—an old one at that."

"Right. What you're looking at is actually a page out of an old *Chicago Sun-Times* newspaper." She scrolled the screen to a particular paragraph. "There, just as I remembered," she said under her breath. "That has to be the answer!"

"The answer to what?" Colby leaned closer. Rita wasn't sure which discovery excited her more—the story in the newspaper column or Colby's warm breath on her ear.

She took a deep inhalation and plunged on. "According to the date, what you're looking at was printed about fifteen years ago." She bent over the keyboard. "The column I'm highlighting now is part of a report of a case that had just been heard in court. It looks as if a relative of a member of the city's business-licensing department was cited for running an employment agency called the Helping Hand Placement Agency."

"That's illegal in Chicago?"

"It is if the personnel you're trying to place are illegal immigrants," Rita said.

Colby thought fast. What he was looking at wasn't news to him, but he didn't want to have to explain how he knew or to burst Rita's bubble. "Interesting."

"Very," Rita agreed. "Especially since the guy who ran the agency was a close relative of the judge," Rita added as she continued to scroll down the page. "It says there that the case was thrown out of court because of hearsay evidence. As far as I can tell from checking ahead, the case was closed. If you ask me," she went on, pointing to the line in the text that identified the agency, "I'll bet the agency is still operating on some level or another, probably under another name."

Afraid of the prospect of Rita's becoming more deeply involved than ever if he admitted she was right on target, Colby said, "Ri, this stuff is interesting, but it isn't something you should get involved in. Besides, there have to be hundreds of employment agencies in Chicago."

"Give me a few minutes and I'll find out." Rita entered "Chicago employment agencies" into an Internet search engine and settled down to see if the right one would turn up.

The sound of her office door opening interrupted them. To Colby's chagrin, a uniformed maintenance man, broom in hand, was standing there. "Oops, sorry," he said. "I thought everyone had gone home. I'll just clean up next door and come back later."

"Damn," Colby said when the worker disappeared.

Rita scowled. "What's wrong?"

"I think the guy saw what was on the monitor."

Rita sniffed. "Now whose imagination is working overtime? We've had a regular maintenance crew around here for ages."

"That guy? You recognize him?" Colby said as he ignored the sniff. Whatever changes Rita had undergone since Sunrise, her stubborn streak was still there stronger than ever.

Rita frowned. "I don't know. I've never paid much attention to the maintenance crew."

"Never mind," Colby muttered, afraid that the major pieces of the puzzle that had brought him to Chicago might fall into place for Rita. The pieces had already come together for him, or he wouldn't have been in Chicago representing the Texas Rangers' interest in the problem in the first place.

What Colby wasn't prepared to do was tell Rita that he'd already heard about the Helping Hand Placement Agency from the Chicago Police Department and the local INS agents. Or that he'd gone underground to check out a clue about the employment agency's illegal operations during the two days he'd been away.

He sure as heck wasn't going to remind her that the employment agency's logo, a human hand, had been on the uniform worn by the would-be maintenance man who'd entered her office a minute ago.

Now, to call her off. "I know where to find the answers. Anyway, whatever it's going to take to finish the job, I don't want you involved any more than you already are."

When Rita started to protest, Colby closed down her computer and then urged her out the door. "Let's go. Now! Let me do the worrying—that's what I get paid for. If there's anything you need to take with you, grab it. I'm taking you home."

What he did wish was that he didn't have to tell Rita he'd come back only to say goodbye before he went underground again, into the murky criminal world. Especially not when he wasn't sure he'd live to come back again.

If only he could tell Rita how he felt about her. But he couldn't. Not now, and maybe never.

Rita glanced at her watch. "It's still early. I'm under a deadline here. I have to finish my part of the historical article on old-time Chicago. Do you want me fired?"

"No," Colby said, trying his best to be patient. He was sure the sinister appearance of his enemies had been only a warning until now. He wasn't about to bet on what would happen next.

"Be reasonable," he finally said. "I've been trying to get you to understand that your home is safer than it is around here—at least for now. The way things are shaping up," he added with a quick glance through the glass office partition, "I'm afraid you'll wind up being the target, as well as me. So let me get you home so you can relax. I'll take over from there."

Rita's mouth set in a stubborn line. "Does that mean you're going to stay in Chicago?"

"Only long enough to get the job done." Colby shot a cautious look down the hall. He wasn't surprised to find that the maintenance worker had disappeared. The question was, where had he disappeared to?

"Give me your boss's telephone number. After I get you home, I promise I'll call and explain to Tom why you not only had to leave early, but that it would be a good idea for you to stay out of sight for a few days."

"Not until you've told me everything," Rita retorted. "You're just trying to get rid of me. Now talk!"

Colby wanted to shake some sense into her, but he knew it would be a waste of precious time. "Will you go home to Sunrise for Christmas if I do?"

Rita glowered at him. "No, of course not! Don't change the subject. I want to know everything that's going on here and now. You owe me. You might have forgotten that I saved your life, but I haven't."

Colby bit his lip. Sure, Rita was convinced she'd saved his life by recognizing men trailing him. He was grateful, but he would have felt a lot better if she hadn't gotten herself involved. His immediate problem appeared to be if he couldn't convince her to get out of his affairs, he'd probably wind up having to save *her*. The thought left him cold.

The thought that serious trouble might break out any minute now—he was convinced that the maintenance worker who had spotted them was not what he appeared to be—left him colder.

One way or another, now that the wrong people had spotted Rita with him, he intended to get her out of sight, come hell or high water.

"Like I said, we'll finish this conversation later. Now, grab what you need to take and let's get out of here." He took her arm and pulled her out of the office as soon as she had her purse. "Yeah, you're right about my attitude," he went on. "I guess this is what you could call the Sullivan side of me. I'm not trying to patronize you. There's a time for a man to protect his woman and the time is now."

His woman! Rita left off her complaints and meekly followed Colby to the elevator.

To Colby's relief, they reached the parking garage without incident. After a pause to search the area for suspicious characters, Colby hurried her toward her car.

"Inside," he ordered. "No, not a peep," he said when Rita opened her mouth to protest again, "not until we get you home. If you still have something to say, you can say it there."

To his surprise, instead of putting up a fuss, Rita slid across the seat and actually smiled at him. If he didn't know better, he would have thought taking her home was not only okay with her, it had been her idea.

"Good. Now take a deep breath and try to relax,"

he said as he glanced around him. "You might not thank me now, but you will later."

He pulled out of the garage and was about to turn onto the street when it happened. A series of sharp staccato sounds and a sharp pain in his shoulder. He'd been shot.

He put a hand on her head and pushed her down out of sight. At the same time, he felt something warm and wet trickle down his forehead. Blood!

"What in heaven's name are you doing?" Rita hollered from the floor.

Colby didn't stop to reply. Through the shock of realizing he'd been shot, not once, but twice, he hit the gas and raced down the street without stopping, then made a left turn to Lakeshore Drive on two wheels.

If he'd been alone, he would have turned the car around and followed the guy who'd shot him, but Rita's safety came first. Getting shot was bad enough, but he wouldn't have been able to live with himself if someone had managed to take her down.

By the time they reached Rita's apartment and he'd parked the car, Colby was more alarmed about her safety than ever. If the dealers in human traffic knew where Rita worked, sure as hell they knew where she lived.

It was just a matter of time before whoever had shot him showed up to finish the job.

Getting shot in the line of duty was one thing, he

thought dimly. Getting shot just when he'd finally realized how much Rita meant to him was unbearable.

Gritting his teeth, he urged Rita out of the car, and by sheer determination hurried her into the building and up to the door of her apartment.

Rita opened the door and turned back to him. "Colby, you've been shot! You have to come inside. I can…"

But Colby didn't hear her. The world began to spin and his knees sagged.

The last thing he remembered was Rita's horrified look as the floor came up to hit him in the face.

Chapter Thirteen

"Colby! Colby Callahan! Don't you dare die on me! If you do, I'll never forgive you!"

He didn't move.

"Come on, you're breathing!" Rita hollered in his ear. "Open your eyes!

The anger in Rita's voice awakened him from the stupor he was in. Too groggy to answer, he tried to remember what had happened and where he was now. A bleary glance through half-open eyes told him he was lying on the floor just inside Rita's apartment, his head in her lap. His left arm was throbbing.

As for Rita, when she wasn't dabbing a cold, wet washcloth to his forehead and ordering him not to die, she was covering his face with kisses. In between the kisses, she was telling him off for not heading for the nearest emergency room, instead of her apartment.

"You're right. I'm sorry," he whispered, before darkness claimed him again.

THE SENSATION OF COLD steel against his bare skin shocked Colby into wakefulness again. It took him a minute to realize that he was still lying on the floor, but now his head was resting on a pillow.

"That's better," Rita murmured as his eyes opened. "How are you feeling?"

He raised his head, peered down at himself and mentally inventoried the parts of his body. "Why am I here in your apartment and not in a hospital room?"

"Because you begged me not to call 911, that's why," Rita answered indignantly. "You kept repeating the word *undercover,* and I finally decided you meant you didn't want anyone to know you've been shot."

"Good decision," Colby muttered as Rita tenderly stroked the hair out of his eyes. "So then what?"

"I asked my next-door neighbor to take look at you. Norma's a nurse working the night shift at Chicago General. Since she was on her way to work, she only had time for a quick check. When she said your wounds are only flesh wounds and told me what to do to take care of them, I forgot calling 911."

Colby struggled to sit up, only to fall back against the pillow.

"Careful, I'm holding scissors!" Rita warned, waving what he considered a lethal weapon in the air. "I couldn't wake you up to get you to take off your shirt to check how badly you were injured, so I cut the shirt's arm off."

Colby cautiously felt his forehead then checked

his shoulder and chest again. There were streaks of blood on his upper left arm and chest, his forehead ached, but the rest of him seemed to be in good shape. "How bad does it look?"

"Not bad," Rita answered, moving her free hand to tenderly pat him on his good shoulder.

Colby clammed up. Not because he didn't have plenty to say, but because he didn't seem to have the strength to say it. Besides, he thought as he peered up at Rita, he liked her ministrations, liked her warm hand sliding across his bare skin, her breath warming his cheek as she bent over him.

He hadn't felt so helpless in a long time, he thought as he eyed the scissors warily. If Rita intended to make him pay in some way for his idiocy in getting her involved in his undercover mission, now would be a good time, he thought, surprised by his black humor.

"The wounds aren't deep at all," she said, "and you're not a bleeder. The bullets seemed to have just grazed you. Now lie still. Norma told me to wash your arm with soap and warm water to disinfect the wounds. Your forehead looks okay now, but I warn you, if your arm doesn't look any better than this in the morning, I'm going to take you to the hospital, whether you want to go or not."

"Are you sure you know what you're doing?" Colby shivered as she attacked what was left of his bloody shirt with the cold scissors.

"If you remember, I did this lots of times when I

was helping Mom patch up my brothers," she murmured. "Now stay still." Her tongue peeked through her teeth as she concentrated on cutting away his shirt.

"If I forgot to thank you," he said, "I'd like to do it now."

"You're welcome." She patted him on the shoulder again. "Now, hold still—there, that does it!" Rita tossed the remaining pieces of his shirt onto a pile of newspapers and adjusted the pillow under his head. "Wait here and don't move. I'll be back in a minute."

Colby nodded and the room swam around him. The way he was feeling, he couldn't have moved even if he'd wanted to.

In minutes Rita was back with a basin of warm, soapy water and a roll of bandages. He held his breath while she went to work bathing his upper arm.

As Rita gently cleaned away the blood, her thoughts turned to the times she'd yearned to run her hands over that solid, muscular chest, to have his arms around her making love to her. To feel the warmth of his body against her own.

Colby was the only man who'd ever stirred her that way, she realized as her gaze locked with his. If only, she thought wistfully as she set the basin of bloodied water aside, she could be sure he felt the same way about her. If he did, then shot or not, she would have taken him in her arms and shown him just how much he meant to her....

Colby winced when Rita applied disinfectant to

his arm, then sighed with disappointment when she wrapped his arm in gauze and her tender care appeared to be over. He forced himself to stay awake, just in case anything else happened. He couldn't stop worrying about Rita. Since he'd driven an identifiable car with her at his side, there was a distinct possibility that someone from the Helping Hand Placement Agency might show up to finish the job the gunman had started.

He should have been savvy enough to use a taxi, not her car. In spite of all the basic rules he'd learned at the Ranger academy, he'd allowed his attraction for Rita to get in the way of his professional thinking. If the appearance of the two men at the restaurants and Navy Pier hadn't been enough to tell him his cover was shot to hell, that "visit" to her office by the Helping Hand worker had been a not-too-subtle reminder his cover had been blown. The shots had confirmed it. Next time they might be fatal.

A hell of a lawman he'd turned out to be.

Rita came back and stood there gazing down at him sympathetically. "How do you feel now?"

Colby struggled to sit up. "I've felt better."

"Maybe you ought to stay here tonight," she said worriedly as she knelt and checked out his forehead and his arm. "You're warm. Maybe we should wait and see how you feel in the morning before you think of leaving."

"Good idea." Privately, Colby knew he was in no

condition to go anywhere even if he'd wanted to. Considering Rita's tender loving care, no chance he wanted to.

"Now," she said briskly, "if you think you can sit up, I'll help you get into bed. Slowly," she cautioned when he began to move. "You're going to feel weak for a bit. You need to rest."

"Sounds good to me," Colby said as he struggled to sit up. He peered around the small studio apartment. "Where's the bedroom?"

"There isn't one, remember? The couch opens up into a queen-size bed." Rita put her arms under his shoulders, hoisted him into an upright position and propped him against an upholstered armchair. "The couch doesn't look like much now, but actually it's quite comfortable. And when you lie there, you can see out the window. I love looking at the stars at night."

"Better than the stars I'm seeing right now," Colby muttered. He took a few deep breaths to clear his mind, then, seeing the worry lines on Rita's forehead, said, "On the other hand, you don't need to have me to care for. Maybe I'd better leave. Just call me a cab—"

"You're not going anywhere!" Rita fixed him with a firm look. "Now hang on, I'll have the bed opened in a jiffy."

"I could use something to drink," he pleaded when the bed was open. "Preferably something strong to help me forget how stupid I was."

"I know just the thing," Rita said as she plumped a pillow and turned down the bedcovers. "A hot toddy made of tea and a liberal addition of brandy. My dad swears it's better than any medicine."

"I'll bet," Colby said as he recalled Rita's old-fashioned father and mother, who both believed in the old folk remedies. Colby was glad of it now.

"In the meantime, try to get the rest of your clothes off. Your slacks have blood on them. I'll rinse them with cold water while you're resting."

Colby smothered a grin. The last time he'd been told to take his pants off had been when he'd had a series of shots administered by an unsympathetic medic. To say that tonight was different was a huge understatement.

Moments later, he heard the whistle of the kettle and the sound of Rita preparing things in the kitchen. The scent of hot tea and brandy filled the air.

By the time she returned to Colby's side, he'd managed to get himself onto the edge of the bed and was trying to slide under the blankets.

"Here, let me help you." Rita set the toddy on the end table and lifted the blankets. Once he was under them, she put pillows behind his back.

"Here you go." She blew across the surface of the hot toddy in an effort to cool it and put an arm around his shoulders. "Sip slowly," she murmured and held the cup to his lips.

"Smells good." Colby took a tentative sip,

breathed a sigh of relief, then took another. "Tastes good, too." He guided the hand holding the cup to her lips. "Frankly, after what I've put you through, you look as if you can use some of this toddy, too. Go ahead."

Rita dipped her head, sipped from the cup, then closed her eyes as the hot drink made its way down to her middle, taking the last of her fears about Colby's injuries with it. "This *does* taste good. Dad never let me drink unless I was sick. I guess he suspected modern medicine would kill me—that made my drinking liquor legit. Even my mother approved of a little brandy in hot tea mixed with sugar when I had a cold."

"I remember." Colby grinned. "It depends on what ails you." Colby took the cup out of Rita's hand, set it on the lamp table beside the couch and pulled her head down to his. "What has been really ailing me," he said softly, "is you."

Rita smiled into his eyes. This was the man who'd made her heart sing years ago and was making her heart sing now. "That's the hot toddy working. I guess Dad was right when he said it's guaranteed to cure what ails you."

"Not for this," Colby whispered as he drew her, unresisting, onto the mattress beside him. "I'm afraid the only one who can cure what ails me right now is not the hot toddy. It's you. How about it, Doc?"

"Colby, your arm!"

"What arm?" Colby said, nuzzling her hair, then her lips as he held her with his good arm. "Brandy must be working already. I've never felt better in my life."

His warm lips reached the base of her throat. She shivered with pleasure. "You're not going to like yourself later when you realize this isn't the real you talking."

"Shush," he murmured. "Don't talk. Just let yourself feel."

She shook her head. "Maybe you'd better go to sleep before your wounds start bleeding again."

"What wounds?" Colby started to unbutton her blouse with his free hand.

Even as she felt a bolt of desire shoot through her, Rita covered his hand with hers. "I'm afraid that's still the brandy talking."

"Trust me, this comes straight from the heart," Colby answered. He took her hand and placed it over his chest. "Feel that if you don't believe me."

Rita's senses swam at the feel of his hammering heart. Visions of what could have happened to him if he'd been shot in the chest, instead of just being grazed in the forehead and arm, drove any doubt about her feelings for Colby out of her mind. Colby was the man she wanted, the man she loved. She leaned into his searching lips.

Rita shuddered with excitement at his kiss. When his warm lips moved to her throat, he said tenderly, "It may have taken getting shot to wake me up, but

I care for the beautiful woman you've become." He punctuated his words with kisses to her neck, her cheeks, her lips.

At the sound of her murmured pleasure, Colby paused and added, "I promise you'll never have reason to complain about my treating you like a kid again."

Rita's heart sang. She gazed into Colby's dark eyes and gently pushed his cowlick away from the wound on his forehead. She'd waited until she found the man of her dreams before she'd decided to give herself; there wasn't a need to wait any longer. She feathered his face, then his chest with kisses.

"Hey," he whispered, "if I had to take off my clothes, so do you." He smiled. "Fair is fair."

As if in a dream, Rita threw any doubts about a future together with Colby to the winds. He was the man with whom she wanted to share her first experience in lovemaking. She nodded and finished unbuttoning her blouse. When she reached behind her to undo her bra, Colby stayed her hand. "Let me," he whispered.

Colby searched her eyes for consent. When she smiled openly, he undid her bra, then helped her push her slacks down over her hips. Soon she was freed of all but her panties. He caressed her waist, then her breasts with his hand until she shivered. "Oh, my," she whispered as she melted into his arm.

"Me, too," he said with a shaky laugh. "Where have you been hiding all this time, Rita Rosales?"

"Waiting for you," she whispered as desire surged through her.

Suddenly Colby pulled away and sank back onto the bed. He heaved an exhausted sigh, which turned into a groan. "I don't know what's wrong with me, Rita, but I can't seem to keep my eyes open. Even when I have the most desirable woman in the world in my arms. Go figure."

Rita smothered a laugh and held Colby's weary body close. "Must be the extra brandy I put into that toddy. Go to sleep," she whispered softly into his hair. "There's always tomorrow morning."

"I'm not going to sleep unless you promise to stay right here beside me," Colby said as the last of his strength ebbed and the room began to dim. Not only from grazing bullets, he knew, not only from the brandy, but because he'd been so busy trying to keep Rita from becoming involved in his mission and at the same time working with the Chicago police that he hadn't slept more than a few hours in days. "Promise me you won't go away. I want to know that I'll wake up with you in my arms and..." His voice trailed off.

When she whispered, "I promise," Colby had fallen fast asleep.

"IF THIS IS HEAVEN, I don't want to wake up," Rita heard Colby murmur into her ear.

She glanced at the bedside clock, then snuggled closer into his warmth. "Go back to sleep, it's only two in the morning."

"Thank heaven," Colby murmured, carefully maneuvering her closer to him until they were skin to heated skin. "Spoons," he said contentedly into the nape of her neck. To her delight, his hand started moving south before he stopped.

"Rita?"

"This is no time to stop to ask questions," Rita said with a shaky laugh. "Either you mean business or you don't."

"Don't you want to know what I was about to ask for?" Colby said with a tortured moan. "Maybe I wanted something hot."

"Not at this time in the morning." Rita chuckled. "If a hot toddy is all you can think of, go back to sleep."

"Hot yes, toddy no," he replied, and blew into her ear. "I just wanted to make sure you agreed with what I've been dying to do for hours."

"Oh, yes, I agree," Rita said over her shoulder, nestling closer into the arms that held her. "That is, if you think you're up to it."

Colby smothered a groan. Thank God Rita couldn't see the struggle he was enduring not to make her his before some satisfying foreplay. "I think I can manage—with a little cooperation from you."

If only Colby knew that in spite of all their teasing talk, how cooperative she felt, he'd be surprised. She turned in his arms to meet his smiling eyes. She'd been dreaming of this moment long enough to be *very* cooperative.

"I hope you don't believe I've been planning this all along or that I'm into casual sex," he said fervently as he brushed her flushed cheeks with his lips. " I want much more from you."

"You wouldn't be here now if I didn't think so," she murmured. "Actually, since this is the first time for me, I'm glad it's you."

Colby drew back as her meaning sank in. "The first time?"

He lifted her chin with a finger so he could look into her eyes. "You were engaged to be married twice," he said as the truth hit him. "Are you telling me you're a virgin?"

Rita nodded.

Colby realized he cared too much for Rita to take her virginity. He held her close a moment before he reluctantly let her go. "I'm sorry, Ri. As much as I want to make love to you, it wouldn't be fair to you— not for your first time. You deserve a man who will always be there for you. Since I have to go back to Texas, I'm not that man."

Rita was stunned. But how could she tell Colby without sounding naive he *was* that man and that this was the one moment she'd been waiting for all her adult life to experience lovemaking?

She told her aching heart that she should be pleased Colby knew her well enough to know that casual sex wasn't her style. But dammit, she wanted to make love with him because she cared for him.

"Come on, Rita," Colby said into her silence. "Now that I've cooled down, I have to tell you this isn't easy for me. I'm trying to tell you that I care too much for you to be your first. Even if you wind up thinking I'm an ass, this—" he gestured at her nakedness "—didn't start out as a casual encounter for me."

Wordlessly, Rita shook her head. Tears pooled in her eyes.

He decided to tell her just enough of the truth about how he felt about her to dry her tears, and still not reveal that he actually loved her. "While I care for you more than any woman I've ever known, I'm not the man you deserve. You deserve someone like your father, a nine-to-five, old-fashioned man who loves one woman for the rest of his life. A man who will cherish you, give you children and a lifetime of knowing he'll always be there for you. As much as I'd like to, I can't be that man."

Rita was shocked at how well he seemed to know her. How could she tell him he was wrong about her when he was so right? How could she try to convince him how much she wanted to be his lover when he'd told her he wasn't interested in a lasting relationship?

"You're right," she finally said, willing away her

tears. "But what I don't understand is why you waited until we were in bed together and I told you I was a virgin before you thought to tell me you're not the man for me."

Colby wanted to take Rita back in his arms, to show her that deep inside he would have liked to be the man for her. He wanted to tell her that his initial interest in her had turned into a love he'd never expected to find. To tell her that the feel of her warm skin against his own, the womanly scent of her, made it hard for him to be so honorable.

He couldn't, not when her life could be at stake if their relationship continued.

"Let's face it, Rita darling," he said with a kiss on the tip of her nose, "you're an incredibly irresistible woman. It never occurred to me that you were still an innocent. I should have guessed."

"What you mean is, I'm a dinosaur," Rita said with a catch in her voice. "A woman like me belongs in a museum."

"Not so," Colby replied as he uttered the words he knew he would carry for the rest of his life. "Any man in his right mind would be proud to have you for the woman he comes home to, to mother his children."

"But not you?" The pain in Rita's eyes hit him square in the gut.

Colby shook his head. He'd managed to hurt her, even though that had been the last thing he'd wanted to do. "I'm truly sorry, Ri. I can't see myself as anyone other than a lawman. Just as I can't see you leaving Chicago to follow me back to Texas. Not after listening to how you feel about going home to Sunrise."

Being a Texas Ranger was a full-time job, and sometimes, as now, life-threatening. He thought of his mother's anguish when his father had been downed in the line of duty. He couldn't bring Rita the same pain.

If he'd had any doubts about the danger of the mission he was on and how it affected her, the past few days had shown him he might have already put Rita's life in jeopardy. If he stayed with her much longer, *still* might.

What hurt even more than his rejection, Rita thought, was that he hadn't given her a chance to make a choice of staying in Chicago while he returned to Texas or to ask her to go with him.

Too proud to share her unhappy thoughts, Rita gathered a blanket around her, slid out of bed and stood staring down at Colby. "Everything I said about Texas was last week," she said slowly. "After these past few days with you, I've changed my mind about a lot of things, including Texas. Including you. I…" Fresh tears welled up in her eyes and she couldn't go on.

His strength returning at the sight of Rita's unhappiness, Colby swung his legs out of bed. He had to get her to listen to reason. He had to make her understand his walking out of her life was for *her* sake, not his. He had to go back underground and finish the duty he'd sworn to do.

He couldn't leave Rita with that lost look in her eyes. And he sure couldn't leave without warning her of the danger that surrounded her.

"Come on, Rita," Colby coaxed, and held out his hand. "How about sitting down here beside me for a few minutes while I try to explain?"

Rita backed away from Colby's reach. "You've explained more than enough." She took a deep breath. "You've convinced me you're going back to Texas. But what I don't understand is why you've never asked me how I feel about going with you."

"And if I had?"

Rita gathered the pieces of her clothing scattered by her feet. Then she gazed proudly into Colby's eyes for the last time. "I guess we'll never know now, will we? I think it's best if you *don't* stay the night. I'll call a cab for you."

She had to face the truth. No matter how much she loved Colby, she never wanted to see him again.

Chapter Fourteen

After a largely sleepless night spent arguing with himself and not getting any answers he could live with, Colby rolled out of bed and checked his injuries in the bathroom mirror. Not bad, not bad at all. No pain now, either. He was lucky the wounds were so superficial. After a quick shower and shave, he dressed and called a cab. Thirty minutes later he strode into police headquarters and headed for the man he was reporting to. He knocked sharply on the office door and, without waiting, entered.

Lieutenant Neil Bruner looked up. "Something on your mind?" Colby nodded. "Let's have it."

"I'm through pussyfooting around that damn employment-agency operation," Colby answered. "You and I know where it is, so why are we waiting to close it down?"

Bruner leaned back in his seat and peered at Colby over his glasses. "What brought that on?"

Colby hesitated. If he told Bruner Rita had figured

out the role the Helping Hand Placement Agency played in smuggling illegal immigrants into the United States, he might get her more involved than ever. Still, the fact remained that if *she* figured it out by researching old newspapers, anyone could do it.

"Hell," he snorted, "the fact that the scam runs under cover of a job-placement agency can't be a secret. Not since you and I know about it and certainly the INS does. I want to know what we're waiting for."

Bruner shrugged. "The matter is out of my hands. You know as well as I do that the operation runs out of many cities, not only Chicago. My understanding is that the INS is waiting to coordinate info and close down all the operations at the same time. Otherwise, the word would spread like wildfire and we'd only have to start over again." He stopped to peer at Colby. "What's the rush?"

Colby planted himself in front of Bruner's desk. "Let's just say things have gotten personal."

Bruner shook his head. "Not good enough. Either you spit out what's gotten you riled up or take yourself out of here. I've got work to do."

Colby resisted an urge to swear. "If I tell you, then everyone at headquarters will know!"

"Not if you close the door," Bruner said coolly. "You've got five minutes, starting now."

Colby closed the door and sank into a chair.

Bruner's eyebrows rose. "Well?"

Damn, Colby thought. The more anyone knew

about Rita, the more dangerous it was for her. "I wouldn't be telling you this now except that someone I care about has gotten herself involved in the operation. But I need your word you won't repeat what I tell you."

"*Her?* I thought so. I can't promise, but go ahead. How and why?"

"Unfortunately—" Colby gestured helplessly "—you'd have to know the lady to have the answer to your questions."

Bruner grinned. "Sounds as if this is going to be interesting."

Colby smiled ruefully. "If you knew her, you'd know that's an understatement." He went on to tell Bruner about his connection with Rita, starting with their background in Sunrise, Texas. How she'd managed to figure out the smuggling situation while doing some research. He went on to relate the possible threat to her life. What he didn't say was that he'd realized he'd fallen in love with Rita in the process.

"Sounds pretty serious," Bruner agreed, toying with his glasses. "Still, I can't let you close down the Helping Hand Agency—not without INS approval. You can bet your silver star they're not going to agree."

Colby surged to his feet. "If that's the case, I have no choice. Either I go in now and close the office down before Rita gets hurt or I turn in my badge!"

"Hold on!" Bruner gestured to Colby to sit again. "You can't just quit. You swore an oath when you joined the Rangers. So calm down. I'll arrange for someone to keep an eye on your friend. I think I also know a way for us to compromise here."

SINCE ALL THE information he and other law-enforcement agents had gathered pointed to the Helping Hand Placement Agency as the local headquarters of the smuggling operation, Colby arranged for backup and headed to the west side of Chicago as soon as he left Bruner's office.

The lieutenant's advice, delivered with a take-it-or-leave-it attitude, had been reluctant but clear. Colby was to forget Rita for the moment, play the game Bruner's way and keep what he was about to do to himself.

He'd play it Bruner's way, Colby thought grimly, but only because of Rita. If he'd had his druthers, he'd close the local agency down while the feds took care of the rest. And if it opened again somewhere else, he'd close that operation down, too.

Not only for Rita's sake, he thought grimly, but because he knew that human traffic, including the unfortunates who paid dearly to come to the States—sometimes with their lives—would disappear into the highly populated area, provided they weren't caught and deported first.

The weathered gray building housing the employment agency was located upstairs from a nondescript video-rental shop. From the way it blended into the local landscape, it wouldn't have drawn attention unless someone knew where to look.

Colby did.

A small group of Hispanics, four men, one woman and a small male child hanging on to his mother's hand, were huddled at the foot of wooden stairs located at the side of the building. Their furious escort was shouting at them in Spanish. From where Colby hid in the alley behind the building, he heard the kid start to cry and his mother sob hysterically.

Colby was bilingual, a requirement for all Texas Rangers, and so he knew that the man was demanding more money from the group; if they didn't produce it, he'd turn them loose to survive by themselves. From what he could make out of the excited replies, the illegals were claiming they not only had no money, they had no relatives in Chicago they could ask to help. Nevertheless, the man continued to harangue them.

Without funds, and obviously unable to understand or speak English, the group, Colby figured, didn't have a prayer of surviving in Chicago. Worse yet, they'd been disposed of by the very people they'd paid to bring them here. Experience had shown Colby the would-be job seekers would be lucky if they lived long enough for the INS to return them to their native countries.

The adults could probably take care of themselves in the long run, but the helpless sound of the child's crying decided him to take action before it was too late.

With his backup expected at any moment, he was going in.

Speaking rapidly in Spanish, he strode to the group. The immigrants froze for a moment, then hurriedly moved away from the stairs at his barked order. Their escort, a man Colby recognized from his time at Navy Pier, was swearing at them.

Colby flipped open his jacket to reveal his Texas Ranger badge and his gun. "I don't want to frighten these people, *señor*," he said with a smile that didn't reach his eyes, "so I'm going to speak to you in English. Understand?"

The man cursed. If Colby hadn't promised Bruner to scare the man into leaving Rita alone, instead of taking him in, Colby would have decked the guy.

The man nodded, venom spilling from his eyes.

"Good." Colby went on, slowly and deliberately. "I'm going to make this quick and easy. Do you know who I am?"

"*Sí,*" the man answered reluctantly.

"Good," Colby said again. Before the man could move, Colby had the guy's arm in a hammerlock behind his back. He applied just enough pressure to make him groan.

With his free hand, Colby grimly reached beneath the man's coat and took out the gun protruding from his belt. "Now, where's your partner?"

The man shrugged. "Who knows?"

Colby applied pressure to the man's arm. "Try again."

"Working," the man said.

"Not good enough," Colby snapped, adding pressure to the hammerlock. "Where is he working?"

With a sneer, the man grunted. "It is too late, *amigo*. Esteban is taking care of your woman."

Colby's blood ran cold. He dropped the man's arm and motioned to the street. "Get the hell out of here before I change my mind," he told him. When he hesitated, Colby added softly, "I promise you you're going to end up not breathing if I do."

With the threat, the man cursed and took off down the street as if the devil were on his heels. Colby bolted for his car.

Rita!

He pulled out his cell phone and made a call to Bruner. "I'm on my way to Rita's office. I think I've scared this SOB into staying away from her, but I'm worried about what his partner is doing. And by the way, send someone out here right away. I have a group of people who need to go to a shelter."

"Why?" Colby glanced at the Christmas decorations on the video-store windows before he pulled away from the curb and stomped on the gas. "Because it's almost Christmas. You know, peace on earth and goodwill to men and all that jazz."

IT WAS CLOSE TO FIVE when Lili walked into Rita's office. "You didn't come down to the cafeteria for the special Christmas lunch they were serving today," she said. "I was sure you would. This is the first chance I've had this afternoon to talk to you. Is everything okay?" When Rita didn't answer right away, Lili went on, "You have seemed sad for a week."

Rita looked up from her computer screen. "Hi, Lili." Lili had had enough unhappiness of her own to handle—she didn't need to hear hers. "Sorry, I should have called to tell you or April I wouldn't be there. I wasn't hungry."

Lili hesitated in the doorway of Rita's office. The worry line creasing her forehead deepened. "Are you not feeling well?"

Sick at heart, Rita would have answered if she hadn't wanted to keep her friend from worrying about her any more than she already was. Losing Colby at the very moment she realized he was the man she'd been waiting for all her life was hard to explain to herself, let alone to someone else. "Actually, I was too busy to break for lunch."

Lili still hesitated. "Are you too busy to spend a few minutes talking to me?"

Rita smothered a yes. Surely, the petite Frenchwoman, the mother of two small children and a woman who'd known tragedy in the premature loss of her husband, would understand Rita's unhappiness. Outwardly shy and demure, Lili was the type who, if she sensed someone was hurting, never walked away without trying to heal the hurt.

If ever Rita needed someone who understood heartache, it was now.

"I'm never too busy for you, Lili." Rita motioned her into the office just as Arthur heaved into view with his refreshment cart. "Arthur's right behind you. We can have tea while we talk."

"Hi, ladies." Ever cheerful, Arthur grinned as he rolled his cart into Rita's office. "What can I get for you this afternoon? Coffee, tea, hot chocolate, a soft drink? Cookies, too, if you're hungry."

"Just tea with lemon for me, thank you. Lili?"

"The same for me," Lili replied.

Rita reached for the cup and saucer Arthur handed her. "By the way, how are you and Alice coming along?"

Arthur blushed. "I gave her a ring the other day."

Reminded of the time she'd put a bug in Arthur's impressionable ear about their co-worker having a secret crush on him, Rita smiled at him. It was nice to know that at least someone was having a happy love life. "When's the wedding?"

Arthur's blush grew deeper. "As soon as we can afford it."

Lili, ever the romantic, clapped her hands. "We have to have a wedding shower for you and Alice!"

Arthur beamed. "Tiffany and a few of the other interns have already told me they're planning one as soon as Alice sets the date."

Rita half listened to the happy exchange between her friend and Arthur while she went back to her computer. The last thing she wanted to think about was a wedding. Especially when it wasn't going to be hers.

Sipping her tea, Lili finally waved Arthur out of the office and turned to Rita. "Now tell me why your eyes are so sad today, yes?"

Rita had to smile at Lili's compassionate gaze. "Yes. It's about Colby, the boy I knew in Texas. Only he's not a boy anymore. He's a man," she added softly.

She went on to tell Lili what had happened from the afternoon Colby had first shown up in her office to the last night, the night he'd left for good. And why. "I thought I knew Colby, but it looks as if I didn't know him, after all."

Lili was silent for a few minutes. "This is the man who appeared on the Paul Horton show with you?" Rita nodded. "He is a fine-looking man. Also, from what you have just told me, an honorable man with honest reasons for going back to Texas, or he wouldn't have left you."

Rita nodded again. "Perhaps, but if Colby had

asked me to go with him, I would have. What hurts so much is that he *didn't* ask me."

"You love this man?"

Rita smiled wistfully. "I'm afraid I do."

"Then you must find him and tell him so, Rita."

Rita shook her head. "I wanted to, but by the time I made up my mind to tell him how I felt, it was too late."

Lili rose to leave. "Then find him and do it now," she said. "A love like this comes only one time," she said with a wistful smile as she blew Rita a kiss goodbye. "This Colby could be yours."

Rita tried to go back to her research but Lili's parting words lingered long after she left.

Lili was right, Rita mused sadly. If only she hadn't been so proud and sent Colby away without letting him explain further why he couldn't make love to her, without her telling him how much she loved him and making him understand how much he meant to her. And, most of all, without telling him she would have followed him anywhere.

She turned off her computer. There was no way she could concentrate on work when she felt so blue, so inadequate. Somewhere in Chicago Colby was trying to help resolve a problem that had evidently plagued the INS for years. If Colby could put his life on the line for a cause he believed in, the least she could do was stand beside him.

Almost unaware of what she was looking at through the glass partition separating her office from the rest of the area, she caught a glimpse of the same maintenance man who'd entered her office the afternoon Colby had been shot. She wouldn't have thought too much about seeing him if the small red feather tucked into the insignia on the shoulder of his uniform hadn't suddenly registered and she remembered Colby's warning.

A chill swept through her. The feather looked the same as the man outside Melvin's Diner had worn in his hatband. The same red feather in the hatbands of the two men at the Navy Pier.

The connection between the incidents became alarmingly clear. The maintenance man had to be part of the illegal-immigration operation!

Before the man could finish cleaning the next office, Rita jumped up to close her door. Her heart hammering in her chest, she reached for the phone, dialed the operator and asked for the Chicago Police Department. She prided herself on being able to take care of herself, but this was one problem she couldn't handle alone.

Just then, the man charged into her office, grabbed the phone out of her hand and pulled her hands behind her back.

"My partner, he call me on his cell phone," the man said inches away from her face. "Your man think he so smart, but it's too late. When he comes, I will take care of both of you!"

"Not too late to show you just how wrong you are!" a male voice behind the man's back thundered.

Before Rita's cursing assailant had a chance to turn around, Colby grabbed him, pulled him away from her and wrestled him to the floor. Seconds later, Colby delivered a punch that knocked the man out.

"Are you okay, Ri?" Breathing heavily, Colby stayed on one knee to catch his breath.

"Thank goodness it's you!" In seconds Colby was on his feet, and Rita fell into his arms. "How did you happen to show up here? How's your arm? Your head?"

"Hang on," Colby said, his eyes on the unconscious man. "Give me a minute while I call for backup."

When he finished the call, he pulled Rita into his arms again and hugged her as if he never wanted to let her go. "My arm and head are fine, thanks to you. I'm here because someone had to give the poor chumps an even break," he said, chuckling. "They wouldn't have stood a chance against you."

Rita wasn't laughing. She'd never felt so frightened. She snuggled farther into Colby's warmth. "You don't have to tell me what you're doing here if you don't want to," she managed to say. "I just want to tell you how grateful I am you showed up."

"Me, too," Colby said.

"I'm telling you now that I'm never going to let you out of my sight again. And when this is over, I'm going to find us a big bed and make love to you. I'll show no mercy."

Colby grinned. "Sounds wonderful."

The maintenance man began to stir. Colby reached into his pocket, and uttering a warning in Spanish, took out a set of handcuffs and cuffed the man. "He'll keep."

"What are you going to do now?" Rita glanced at the man with a shiver.

"We'll wait for backup before we leave. I'll check with the magazine's personnel manager in the morning and find out if the Helping Hand Placement Agency has actually been hired for the building maintenance, or if this was a one-time setup. Don't worry. Either way, I'll take it from there."

"*You'll* take it from there?" Rita said, glancing at the telephone. "I've already called 911. They're sending a man out as soon as they can. He ought to be here at any moment."

"They have already, and I am taking it from here."

At Rita's frown, he explained, "Since I'm already on loan to the Chicago Police Department for the duration of this assignment, I had a heart-to-heart with the detective in charge. When I told him about you, he let me make a few arrangements of my own without waiting for the feds."

"And?"

Colby felt the need to confess he'd been one step ahead of her for a long time. He stood directly in front of her, his hands loosely holding her arms. "When you showed me the newspaper article on the Internet, I should have told you I already knew who the local ringleaders of the operation were and where they were. The truth is, they operate all over the country and there are too many of them to bust right now. I just visited their local headquarters and took care of the other man who threatened you. I don't think he'll bother you again, either."

Rita frowned. "You did that without me?"

"No, sweetheart. Mentally, you were with me every step of the way. Oh, and by the way, since the law is in my blood, I think I should tell you that when this assignment is through, I plan on retiring from the Rangers and joining the Chicago P.D."

Rita stared at him in amazement. "What? You can't—"

"Oh, and one more thing," he interrupted her. "Since I'd already asked the Chicago police to keep an eye on you, the detective in charge sent me here to stay with you until they could furnish you with a bodyguard."

"But…but…I'm flabbergasted," Rita said. "I mean, I'm happy you'll be here in Chicago, but I know how much you love being a Ranger."

Colby squeezed her arms and looked tenderly into her startled eyes. "That was an easy decision, sweet Rita," he said. "I discovered I loved you more."

"You did? You do?" Rita whispered. She still felt flabbergasted by his declaration, but the knowledge that he really loved her seeped deliciously into her system, warming everything in its path. And he was willing to sacrifice his career for her? "You would do that for me?"

"Yes, and I'm happy to do it," Colby said. He glanced out at the deserted area outside her office. "Let's go somewhere where I can show you just how much. Your place or mine?"

"You actually have a place?" Rita asked, her heart beating faster. If there was ever going to be a time to be Colby's, this was it.

"Just my hotel room," Colby answered. "But I think I should tell you it's just a place to sleep. If you choose to go there, I have to tell you there's no window overlooking Lake Michigan. We won't be able to cuddle in bed and look out at the stars. But," he added with a soft smile, "this time, Rita, it's your call."

"In that case, my place," Rita said with a wicked grin. "I not only have that picture window, I'll be able to make you another one of my hot toddies."

"I'm sure I won't need a hot toddy tonight," Colby said as he pulled Rita close. "Not when I've got my love to keep me warm."

Chapter Fifteen

Rita didn't know who reached the couch in her apartment first, but it took the two of them only seconds to open it into a bed.

Rita whipped off her jacket, then paused. "We can help each other take our clothes off."

Colby's eyes glinted. "Ah, lovely idea. But not before…"

All of Rita's nerve ends began to tingle. "Before what?"

He pulled her into his arms and crushed her lips with his. Their bodies were touching from thigh to shoulder, and Rita became aware of a hardness against her stomach.

Just as her head began to swim at the realization of what the hardness was and at the thought of finally belonging to Colby, he kissed her breasts through her blouse. "Sorry, I couldn't wait."

"I can't wait, either," she murmured and kissed him back. This time, with all the pent-up desire in her. "I'm through being sensible," she said. "Twenty-eight years has been long enough." She started to unbutton his shirt, then stopped. "How's your arm?"

"I'd forgotten I was even hit," he replied, opening his arms wide. "Go ahead. Do your worst."

Trying to draw off his clothing while he took hers off, Rita soon had him half-undressed.

"Slow down a minute," he laughed. "I never expected a wrestling match." With each piece of her clothing, he stopped to kiss her again and again and again until all her clothes were gone. Breathless, she fell naked onto the bed, taking Colby with her.

"Tell me what you would like," a suddenly sober Colby whispered against the tingling skin of her neck. "I want your first time to be special."

It wasn't easy to think clearly with Colby's arms holding her, his bare chest crushing her to him, his arousal hot and hard against her. "It's already special," she murmured, "because I'm with *you*. Everything you do with me is special."

"Oh, my darling," he said. "And I want to do *everything* with you. But first, sweetheart…"

He sat up at the edge of the bed and reached for his pants. From a pocket he withdrew a small packet, opened it and sheathed himself. Then he lay back down beside her and brought his fingers to her face, tracing down to her lips, then her throat, her shoulders. By the time he'd reached her waist, where he stopped to lovingly kiss her, Rita knew exactly what she wanted. She wanted him all around her and inside her.

"I want you, all of you!" she cried, and drew his head up to hers. She felt the rapid beating of his heart against her own, breathed in the male scent of him.

Smiling into her eyes, Colby fit himself between her legs and cradled himself in a sensitive place where it seemed she'd waited a lifetime for him to be. His tongue played with her lips, her tongue. His hands caressed her breasts until she was almost mindless with desire.

"I don't want to hurt you," he whispered, "but I'm afraid I will. But only for a moment, I promise."

"Please, please," Rita urged him. "Don't stop."

"Now?" he asked gently, his eyes caressing her at the same time his hands grasped her waist, holding her in place.

"Now," Rita echoed. She put her arms around his neck.

Colby slowly, gently, began to ease into her. "I love you, sweet Rita," he said. "Are you sure?"

"I've never felt surer in my life," Rita said. "And I love you. Oh, how I love you!" Instinctively she lifted her hips to encourage Colby's thrust.

There was the briefest moment of pain, and then it was gone. The full moon that had just come up over Lake Michigan entered the room to shimmer on Colby's shoulders. Up, up and up she felt herself surge, where she seemed to float in a sea of warmth until, in a final burst of pleasure, she fell back into Colby's arms. Never, in her wildest fantasies, had she ever imagined lovemaking could be like this.

"Oh, my," she said into Colby's damp shoulder. She couldn't think of the words to express how deeply happy she felt. So instead she said, "If you don't mind, I'd like to try this again."

He smiled into her eyes. "Happy to, my love, but give me a few minutes." He gestured at the window. "The night's still young. You're right about being able to watch the stars through that window." He looked back at her. "But I'd rather watch you."

Rita blinked happily. Little Ri had finally become Rita.

Colby gathered her close and tucked her head beneath his chin. "I noticed you haven't decorated your little Christmas tree yet."

"I'm afraid my heart wasn't in it."

"Don't worry, we'll decorate it together. In the meantime, I have something important to ask you."

Rita's heart raced. "Ask away."

"I love you, darling Rita. Will you be my wife?" When she whispered "oh my" again, he said, "What do you say?"

Rita did indeed wanted to be Colby's wife, but she hesitated. Knowing him as well as she did, there was no way she wanted him to go through with his plan to leave Texas and his beloved Rangers just for her.

"My answer is yes," she said at last. "And if you

eventually decide to stay with the Rangers and live in Texas, my answer is still yes."

"Are you sure, really sure? I'm willing to live anywhere where you'll be happy."

Rita bent to kiss his chin. "I'm really, really sure, my darling. Besides, I *have* to marry you. I couldn't possibly ruin my mother's belief in the bridal-bouquet superstition, now, could I?"

Colby eyes lit up with laughter. "We can pay your mom a visit over the Christmas holidays. And then we'll come back to Chicago and look for a place for the two of us to live."

"Oh, Colby, you mean it?" Rita breathed. "You'd be happy with Chicago as your home?"

"Home is where the heart is," he murmured into her lips. "And my heart is wherever you are."

* * * * *

Watch for Lili's story,
A Convenient Engagement, *in June 2005.*

*Turn the page for a preview of next month's
American Romance titles!*

*We hope these brief excerpts will whet your
appetite for all four of January's books...*

One Good Man by Charlotte Douglas (#1049) is the second title in this popular author's ongoing series, "A Place to Call Home." Charlotte Douglas creates a wonderful sense of home and community in these stories.

Jeff Davidson eased deeper into the shadows of the gift shop. Thanks to his Special Operations experience, the former Marine shifted his six-foot-two, one-hundred-eighty pounds with undetectable stealth. But his military training offered no tactics to deal with the domestic firefight raging a few feet away.

With a stillness usually reserved for covert insertions into enemy territory, he peered through a narrow slit between the handmade quilts, rustic birdhouses and woven willow baskets that covered the shop's display shelves.

On the other side of the merchandise in the seating area of the café, a slender teenager with a cascade of straight platinum hair yelled at her mother, her words exploding like a barrage from the muzzle of an M-16. "You are so not with it. Everyone I hang with has her navel pierced."

Jeff grimaced in silent disapproval. The kid should

have her butt kicked, using that whiny, know it all tone toward her mom. Not that the girl's behavior was his business. He hadn't intended to eavesdrop. He'd come to Mountain Crafts and Café to talk business with Jodie Nathan, the owner, after her restaurant closed. Lingering until the staff left, he'd browsed the shelves of the gift section until she was alone.

But before he could make his presence known, fourteen-year-old Brittany had clattered down the stairs from their apartment over the store and confronted her mother.

"Your friends' navels are their mothers' concern, not mine." The struggle for calm was evident in Jodie's firm words, and the tired slump of her pretty shoulders suggested she'd waged this battle too many times. "You are my daughter, and as long as you live under my roof, you will follow my rules."

Was the kid blind? Jeff thought with disgust. Couldn't she see the tenderness and caring in her mother's remarkable hazel eyes? An ancient pain gnawed at his heart. He'd have given everything for such maternal love when he'd been a child, a teenager. Even now. Young Brittany Nathan had no idea how lucky she was.

Daddy by Choice by Marin Thomas (#1050) is a "Fatherhood" story with a Western slant. This exciting new author, who debuted with the delightful *The Cowboy and the Bride*, writes movingly and well about parent-child relationships…and, of course, romance!

JD wasn't sure if it was the bright sunlight bouncing off the petite blond head or the sparkling clean silver rental car that blinded him as he swung his black Ford truck into a parking space outside Lovie's café. Both the lady and the clean car stood out among the dusty, mud-splattered ranch vehicles lined up and down Main Street in Brandt's Corner.

Because of the oppressive West Texas heat wave blanketing the area, he shifted into Park and left the motor running. Without air-conditioning, the interior temperature would spike to a hundred degrees in sixty seconds flat, and he was in no hurry to get out.

He had some lookin' to do first.

A suit in the middle of July? He shook his head at the blonde's outfit. Pinstripe, no less. She wore her honey-colored hair in a fancy twist at the back of her neck, revealing a clean profile. Evidently, she got her haughty air from the high cheekbones.

All of her, from her wardrobe to her attitude, represented a privileged life. Privileged meant money. Money meant trouble.

His gut twisted. Since yesterday's phone call from this woman, his insides had festered as if he'd swallowed a handful of rusty fence nails.

Fear.

Fear of the unknown…the worst kind. He'd rather sit on the back of a rank rodeo bull than go head to head with her. Too bad he didn't have the option.

Table for Five by Kaitlyn Rice (#1051) is an example of our "In the Family" promotion—stories about the joys (and difficulties) of life with extended families. Kaitlyn Rice is a talented writer whose characters will stay with you long after you've finished this book.

Kyle Harper glanced at his watch and uttered a mild curse. He'd worked well past a decent quitting time again—an old habit that was apparently hard to break. Shoving the third-quarter sales reports into his attaché case, he closed his eyes, claiming a few seconds of peace before switching gears. He pictured a perfect gin martini, a late version of the television news and a bundle of hickory wood, already lit and crackling in the fireplace.

Heaven.

Or home, as he'd once known it.

Life didn't slow down for hard-luck times, and it didn't cater to wealth or power. Kyle could afford only a moment to ponder used-to-be's. He popped open his eyes and grabbed his cell phone, the fumbling sounds at the other end warned him about what to expect. "Grab the guns!" Kyle's father yelled. "There's a gang of shoot-'em-up guys headed into town!"

The Forgotten Cowboy by Kara Lennox (#1052) is an unusual take on a popular kind of plot. Thanks to the heroine's amnesia, she doesn't recognize the cowboy in her life—which makes for some interesting and lively complications!

Willow Marsden studied the strange woman in her hospital room. She was an attractive female in her twenties, her beauty marred by a black eye and a bandage wound around her head. The woman looked unfamiliar; she was a complete stranger. Unfortunately, the stranger was in Willow's mirror.

She lay the mirror down with a long sigh. Prosopagnosia—that was the clinical name for her condition. She'd suffered a head injury during a car accident, which had damaged a very specific portion of her brain—the part that enabled humans to distinguish one face from another. For Willow, every face she saw was strange and new to her—even those of her closest friends and relatives.

"You're telling me I could be like this forever?"

Dr. Patel, her neurologist, shrugged helplessly. "Every recovery is different. You could snap back to normal in a matter of days, weeks, months, or…yes, the damage could be permanent."

"What about my short-term memory?" She couldn't even remember what she'd had for breakfast that morning.

Again that shrug. Why was it so difficult to get a straight answer out of a doctor?

Willow knew she should feel grateful to be alive, to be walking and talking with no disfiguring scars. Her car accident during last week's tornado had been a serious one, and she easily could have died if not for the speed and skill of her rescuers. Right now, though, she didn't feel grateful at all. Her plans and dreams were in serious jeopardy.

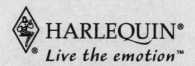

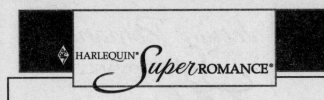

Mother and Child Reunion

A ministeries from
2003 RITA® finalist

Jean Brashear

Coming Home

Cleo Channing's dreams were simple: the stable home and big, loving family she never had as a child. Malcolm Channing walked into her life and swept her off her feet and before long, she thought she had it all—three beautiful children in a charming house she would fill to the rafters with love.

Their firstborn was a troubled girl, though, and the strain on their family grew until finally, there was nothing left to do but for them to all go their separate ways.

Now their daughter has returned, and as the days pass, awareness grows in Cleo and Malcolm that their love never truly died.

Except, the treacherous issues that drove them apart in the first place remain....

Heartwarming stories with a sense of humor, genuine charm and emotion and lots of family!

On sale starting January 2005
Available wherever Harlequin books are sold.

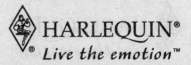

Harlequin Romance®

Contract Brides

From paper marriage...to wedded bliss?

A *wedding dilemma:*

What should a sexy, successful bachelor do if he's too busy
making millions to find a wife? Or if he finds the perfect
woman, and just has to strike a bridal bargain...?

The *perfect proposal:*

The solution? For better, for worse, these grooms in a hurry
have decided to sign, seal and deliver the ultimate
marriage contract...to buy a bride!

Coming Soon to

HARLEQUIN®
Romance®

featuring the favorite miniseries Contract Brides:

THE LAST-MINUTE MARRIAGE
by Marion Lennox, #3832
on sale February 2005

A WIFE ON PAPER
by award-winning author Liz Fielding, #3837
on sale March 2005

VACANCY: WIFE OF CONVENIENCE
by Jessica Steele, #3839
on sale April 2005

Available wherever Harlequin books are sold.

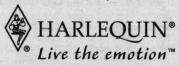

HARLEQUIN®
® *Live the emotion™*

www.eHarlequin.com

If you enjoyed what you just read,
then we've got an offer you can't resist!

Take 2 bestselling love stories FREE!

Plus get a FREE surprise gift!

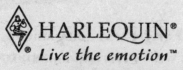

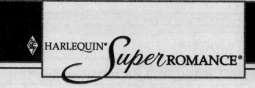

HARLEQUIN® *Super*ROMANCE®

COUNT ON A COP

Forgotten Son by Linda Warren
Superromance #1250
On sale January 2005

Texas Ranger Elijah Coltrane is the forgotten son—the one his father never acknowledged. Eli's half brothers have been trying to get close to him for years, but Eli has stubbornly resisted. That is, until he meets Caroline Whitten, the woman who changes his mind about what it means to be part of a family.

By the author of *A Baby by Christmas* (Superromance #1167).

The Chosen Child by Brenda Mott
Superromance #1257
On sale February 2005

Nikki's sister survived the horrible accident caused by a hit-and-run driver, but the baby she was carrying for Nikki and her husband wasn't so lucky. The baby had been a last hope for the childless couple. Devastated, Nikki and Cody struggle to get past their tragedy. If only Cody could give up his all-consuming vendetta to find the drunk responsible—and make him pay.

Available wherever Harlequin books are sold.

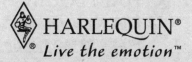

HARLEQUIN®
Live the emotion™

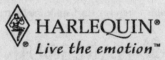